The Cat of Christmas Future

by

Kathi Daley

This book is a work of fiction. Names, characters, places, and incidents either are products of the author's imagination or are used fictitiously. Any resemblance to actual events or locales or persons, living or dead, is entirely coincidental.

Copyright © 2017 by Katherine Daley

Version 1.0

I want to thank the very talented Jessica Fischer for the cover art.

I so appreciate Bruce Curran, who is always ready and willing to answer my cyber questions, and Peggy Hyndman, for helping sleuth out those pesky typos.

A special thank you to Taryn Lee, Nina Banks, Jeannie Daniels, Pamela Curran, Vivian Shane, and Robin Coxon for submitting recipes.

And, of course, thanks to the readers and bloggers in my life, who make doing what I do possible.

Thank you to Randy Ladenheim-Gil for the editing.

And finally I want to thank my sister Christy for always lending an ear and my husband Ken for allowing me time to write by taking care of everything else.

Books by Kathi Daley

Come for the murder, stay for the romance.

Zoe Donovan Cozy Mystery:

Halloween Hijinks
The Trouble With Turkeys
Christmas Crazy
Cupid's Curse
Big Bunny Bump-off
Beach Blanket Barbie
Maui Madness
Derby Divas
Haunted Hamlet
Turkeys, Tuxes, and Tabbies
Christmas Cozy
Alaskan Alliance
Matrimony Meltdown
Soul Surrender
Heavenly Honeymoon
Hopscotch Homicide
Ghostly Graveyard
Santa Sleuth
Shamrock Shenanigans
Kitten Kaboodle
Costume Catastrophe
Candy Cane Caper
Holiday Hangover
Easter Escapade
Camp Carter
Trick or Treason
Reindeer Roundup – *December 2017*

Zimmerman Academy The New Normal
Ashton Falls Cozy Cookbook

Tj Jensen Paradise Lake Mysteries by Henery Press:

Pumpkins in Paradise
Snowmen in Paradise
Bikinis in Paradise
Christmas in Paradise
Puppies in Paradise
Halloween in Paradise
Treasure in Paradise
Fireworks in Paradise
Beaches in Paradise – *June 2018*

Whales and Tails Cozy Mystery:

Romeow and Juliet
The Mad Catter
Grimm's Furry Tail
Much Ado About Felines
Legend of Tabby Hollow
Cat of Christmas Past
A Tale of Two Tabbies
The Great Catsby
Count Catula
The Cat of Christmas Present
A Winter's Tail
The Taming of the Tabby
Frankencat
The Cat of Christmas Future
The Cat of New Orleans – *February 2018*

Seacliff High Mystery:

The Secret
The Curse
The Relic
The Conspiracy
The Grudge
The Shadow
The Haunting

Sand and Sea Hawaiian Mystery:

Murder at Dolphin Bay
Murder at Sunrise Beach
Murder at the Witching Hour
Murder at Christmas
Murder at Turtle Cove
Murder at Water's Edge
Murder at Midnight

Writers' Retreat Southern Seashore Mystery:

First Case
Second Look
Third Strike
Fourth Victim
Fifth Night – *January 2018*

Rescue Alaska Paranormal Mystery:

Finding Justice

A Tess and Tilly Mystery:

The Christmas Letter – *December 2017*

Road to Christmas Romance:

Road to Christmas Past

Chapter 1

Wednesday, December 13

There was, admittedly, more popcorn on the floor than on the tree, but I still considered our night's endeavor to be a success. The annual production of the Christmas story, performed by the children's choir at St. Patrick's Catholic Church, was just nine days away and my fiancé, Cody West, and I were supervising the children who would portray the characters as they decorated the church auditorium in preparation for the throngs of proud parents and grandparents who planned to attend. I'd always loved this season, but it seemed even more special this year as Cody and I discussed traditions and planned our life together.

"Everything looks just perfect," Father Bartholomew complimented us as he walked up behind me.

"Thank you," I said as the song playing in the background changed from "Silent Night" to "The First Noel." "I think it's coming together nicely."

"I especially love the lights around all the windows. They give the whole room a festive feel."

"The kids wanted to go all-out because this will be your first Christmas with us." Father Bartholomew was a young priest who had come to St. Patrick's earlier in the year after our longtime priest, Father Kilian, retired.

"I appreciate how welcome everyone has made me feel. I'll admit to being somewhat nervous about trying to fill Father Kilian's shoes. I'm fairly new at this and he's been such an important fixture in the community for so many years."

"He has," I agreed. "And he'll continue to be a member of the community even in retirement, but we're very happy to have you with us. In fact, I'd like to invite you to the annual Christmas Eve dinner Cody and I prepare for those who may not have other plans over the holiday. It's held at the home of Mr. Parsons, the man Cody lives with and looks out for."

"Why, thank you. I'd enjoy that very much."

"Great," I answered as I placed my hand on the shoulder of one of the boys as he ran past us, tailing a chain of red and green construction paper. I raised an eyebrow at Robby, who got my silent hint to slow down and did so. "I'll get you the address. If you come across any other parishioners who are going to be alone for the holiday, feel free to bring them along. Cody and I want to be sure everyone has somewhere to go."

"Thank you again. That's very kind of you. It warms my heart the way this congregation welcomes newcomers. In fact, there's a newcomer I'd like you to meet." Father Bartholomew waved to a man who had just entered the room. He walked toward us, and the two men shook hands. "Caitlin Hart, I'd like you to meet Richard Sinclair. As I indicated, Richard is new to the island and to St. Pat's."

"I'm happy to meet you, Richard." I shook his hand.

"Please call me Rich."

"Okay, then, nice to meet you, Rich. Most people call me Cait."

"I'm hoping to talk Mr. Sinclair into filling the vacancy we have with the adult choir. He was a member of the choir at the church he previously attended, and I think he'll do quite well in the role of director."

"We could use the help," I seconded.

The tall, dark-haired man with silver streaks paused before he answered. "I told Father Bartholomew I'd consider it, but I have a lot on my plate right now. Still, I'd like to see the facility."

"I have a church council to get to," Father Bartholomew said, "but perhaps Cait could walk you over to the choir room and show you around."

I smiled. "Sure. I'd be happy to. Just let me tell Cody what I'm doing."

I wiped a streak of glitter from my cheek and filled Cody in on my errand, then returned to Rich, motioning for him to follow me. "So, how long have you lived on the island?" I asked conversationally.

"Just a few weeks. I purchased the abandoned warehouse on the east side of the island. I'm planning to renovate it and turn it into a high-end restaurant."

"That's a wonderful location for a restaurant, but I have a feeling you'd be better off tearing the whole thing down and starting over. It's in pretty bad shape."

"Perhaps. My contractor will be here on Monday and we'll have that conversation. If I do tear it down I'd want to repurpose some of the wood. It's aged and rustic, exactly the sort of thing I'm going for."

"What sort of a restaurant are you planning to open?" I asked as we headed across the property toward the main building.

"An upscale Italian restaurant, with an extensive steak-house menu as well. I worked in a similar place when I lived in Seattle and it did quite well."

I paused. "A high-end restaurant might work in Seattle, but Madrona Island is pretty casual. You might want to consider offering some items geared toward our working-class lifestyle. I'm sure you'd attract visitors to the island with a high-end menu, but honestly, I don't think you'd get much business from the locals. Tourism on the island dries up in the winter, so unless you only plan to be open seasonally, you'll need business from the island's residents as well as tourists."

"Thank you for the input. I'll take your comments into consideration when I make up my final menu."

Once we entered the main parish structure, I opened the door to the music room and stepped inside. "Here we are. It's small, but it's home."

"It's nice; I like it," Rich said, entering the room behind me. He took several steps inside, looking around as he went.

"Cody and I practice on Wednesdays and the children's choir services the eleven o'clock Mass on

Sundays. Currently, the adult choir practices on both Tuesdays and Thursdays and performs during both the eight o'clock service on Sunday and the seven-thirty service on Saturday night. If you agree to take over you can discuss the specifics with Father Bartholomew."

"Thank you. I'll definitely think over his offer. I enjoy being part of a choir, but I'm not sure I have time to take the lead. I'll have a lot to do if I want to get the restaurant open by spring, starting with the eviction of the squatters who're living there right now."

I frowned. "There are people living there?"

"Not legally, but the place has been empty for so long that a group of homeless people have set up camp. The first thing I need to do before I can start on the renovation is to convince the resident deputy to kick everyone out."

My heart filled with sympathy for those individuals who would be displaced. "It's Christmas. Can't the eviction wait until after the first of the year?"

"Not if I want to meet my opening deadline." Rich looked around the room. "I know you need to get back to the kids. Would you mind if I stay and poke around a bit?"

"Not at all. I'll be in the auditorium if you need anything."

As I walked back to where Cody and the kids were waiting, a feeling of déjà vu washed over me. Two years ago, Cody and I had been helping the choir kids to decorate on a Wednesday evening when a beautiful cat named Ebenezer showed up. Like tonight, it had been snowing, and like tonight, I'd found out that a local business owner planned to put people out on the street just days before Christmas. Cody and I had been able to stop it then and I wondered if we weren't meant to intervene now. Of course this situation was different. The tenants living in Balthazar Pottage's apartment building had been living there legally and, I felt, had the right to be given additional notice if they had to move. Additionally, Balthazar was a reclusive miser who could well afford to wait a few days to give the tenants time to make other arrangements. I wasn't sure whether Rich Sinclair had the financial means to put off the renovation of the warehouse and I wasn't sure exactly what I could do to stop him from evicting squatters, but I intended to find out exactly who was living in the building. Hopefully, Cody and I could come up with a plan to help them relocate.

"The place looks great," I said when I returned to the auditorium, where red and green lights strung from the ceiling twinkled to the sound of the carols playing in the background. "Very festive."

"I think the kids did a good job. Did you get the new choir director settled?"

"I showed him the room, but I'm less than convinced he's actually going to take on the duties associated with running the choir. He just moved to the island and it sounds like he already has a lot of things to do."

"It's hard to find volunteers who have the time to take on the larger roles."

"Yes, I guess it is. The choir commitment takes a lot of our time, but I wouldn't give it up for anything."

"I agree." Cody smiled. "Speaking of a time commitment, while you were gone the kids asked if we were going to meet more than once next week."

"I think we should. The play is on Saturday, so let's have the kids meet in the choir room on Monday and Wednesday, and then we'll have a dress rehearsal on Friday. I'll go over to Father Bartholomew's office to run off flyers with the dates and times. It would probably be best if we sent the information home tonight."

"Okay. I'll have everyone start cleaning up."

I was halfway back to the main church building where the offices and choir room were located when a cat I knew well ran across the lawn toward me. "Ebenezer, what are you doing here?"

"Meow."

The feeling of déjà vu I'd had minutes before suddenly intensified. I'd first met him on that snowy Wednesday two years ago. Looking back, I knew he'd come to help me with the huge task I'd taken on. I had to wonder if he wasn't here again for a similar purpose.

"It's coming down pretty hard; let's get inside." I picked up the large, furry cat and continued toward the office, where the copier was kept. I should probably try to contact Balthazar to let him know I had his cat. Ebenezer seemed to come and go as he pleased, but I knew the old man was firmly attached to him and thought he might worry if he was gone too long without a word.

I set Ebenezer on the floor while I grabbed a Sharpie and penned a note with the dates and times of practice the following week. Then I placed the paper on the copier and pressed the button to make thirty copies, which would be more than enough. I was waiting for the ancient machine to crank them out when I heard a voice raised in anger. The voice sounded like Rich's and seemed to be coming from down the hall. I supposed he could still be in the choir room, but who was in there with him? Whatever was going on was none of my business and I probably shouldn't listen, but I couldn't seem to quell my natural curiosity and found myself inching toward the partially open door.

"I don't care what you have to do to get them out, just do it."

The voice, which I confirmed did belong to Rich, paused. When I didn't hear a response I assumed he was on the phone.

"Yes, even the girl. I know her situation, but the fact that she's homeless and pregnant isn't my problem. I have a contractor coming to the island on Monday. If the place isn't empty by then heads are going to roll."

Yikes. The situation sounded worse than I'd thought. Monday was just five days away, not a lot of time to relocate a bunch of people. I grabbed the stack of copies I'd made and headed back to the auditorium. Once the kids had been picked up I'd share what I knew with Cody. Maybe between the two of us we could come up with at least a temporary solution.

"I have the rehearsal schedule," I held up the flyers.

"Great." Cody took them from me. He turned and looked at the kids, who had gathered their possessions in preparation for pickup. "I have flyers I need each of you to give to a parent. We'll be having extra rehearsals next week as we prepare for our performance and I need everyone to attend every rehearsal."

The kids, who were thrilled to see Ebenezer had come for a visit, played with the cat and chatted among themselves as Cody passed out the flyers. Parents had begun to arrive and I wanted to be sure all of them had the information, so I stood at the door to catch anyone who might not have received one.

"I have a rehearsal schedule for next week," I said to one of the moms, whose son was messing around and hadn't taken a flyer.

"Great." She smiled. "I was wondering if you were going to have extra rehearsals. I hear congratulations are in order. Have you set the date?"

"Thank you and not yet. Cody and I decided to wait until after the first of the year to discuss specifics. There's so much going on right now, everything seems a bit overwhelming."

She placed her hand on my arm. "I don't blame you for taking your time. When I got engaged I was so excited I bought a dress the very next day. Over the course of the next nine months I planned a huge wedding and was stressed the entire time. If I had it to do over again I'd take my time and plan something special to us, not just something big and flashy."

"We feel the same way. We have a lot of family and friends, so I'm not sure small will work, but I'm definitely thinking simple."

"It sounds like you have the beginnings of a plan." The woman looked around the room, located her son, and waved him over. "We should get going. Congratulations again."

I thanked her and moved on to the next parent who seemed to be lacking a flyer. Once the kids had all been delivered to their parents, Cody and I cleaned up and headed, along with Ebenezer, to my cabin. I filled him in on what I knew of the warehouse situation as we drove.

Cody being the smart and wonderful man he is jumped right in with an idea. "I think the first thing we need to do is find out exactly who's living in the building and what their situation is. There may be people who have a place to go if provided with the means to get there, and others who have a long-term plan and only require short-term housing. I think I can work out a deal with the motor lodge for short-term housing if needed. We'll drive out there first thing in the morning and figure out what's what."

"Okay, that sounds great." I glanced at Ebenezer, who was sitting on the seat between us. "I should go talk to Balthazar as well. He owns several apartment buildings. Maybe he'd be willing to help out if he has vacancies."

"We can see him tomorrow after we visit the warehouse."

"Don't you have that guy coming from the ad agency tomorrow?" I asked.

Cody grimaced. "I do; I almost forgot. He isn't coming until eleven, though, so we can still visit the warehouse in the morning. We can see Balthazar the following day, or you can catch the morning ferry and go on your own tomorrow."

"I'll go alone. Ebenezer can come with me. If Rich is serious about having everyone out by Monday we don't have time to waste."

"You should let Finn know what's going on too," Cody said, referring to my brother-in-law, who happened to be the island's resident deputy. "If Sinclair plans to use force to get the squatters out Finn can ensure that things are handled legally and without violence."

"Good idea. I'll call him when we get to the cabin." I glanced out the window at the still-falling snow. "I know we talked about going out for dinner on the way home, but I think we should head back before the roads get bad. I've got some soup left over from last night and another loaf of bread in the freezer."

"Sounds good. I want to pop in to check on Mr. Parsons. I'll drop you and Ebenezer off at your place, check on him, and then come back to the cabin."

It did my heart good to see how much Cody cared for the elderly man he shared a space with. There'd been a time when Mr. Parsons was a bit of a grump, but ever since Cody had remodeled and moved into the third floor of his huge oceanfront mansion, Mr. Parsons had let go of his anxiety, and almost everyone agreed he was a changed man.

After Cody dropped Ebenezer and me off I took my dog Max out for a quick run, then got our houseguest set up with kitty food and a cat box. When both animals were fed and settled I called Finn. He didn't answer his cell, so I tried the house.

"Oh, hey, Siobhan," I greeted my sister when she answered the phone. "I'm looking for Finn, but he didn't answer his cell."

"He's out on a call. There's a pretty bad accident along the west shore."

"Oh no. I'm so sorry to hear that. Were there injuries?"

"I don't know," Siobhan said. "I haven't heard. I hope not."

"Yeah, me too. I love the snow, but there's always an increase in auto accidents when the roads are icy."

"People don't want to slow down."

"So, how's the packing going?" I asked. Finn and Siobhan had sold Finn's house and bought a larger one together.

"It's been hectic. This place closes in just a few days and we need to be completely moved out by the end of the weekend."

"Don't overdo," I warned my pregnant sister.

"I'm trying not to, but everything is going so fast. It's a bit overwhelming, and to make matters worse, there seems to be a problem with the house we're buying."

I frowned. "Problem? What sort of problem?"

"It seems the woman who's selling it is getting cold feet. To be honest, I've been wondering if that house was the right one for us anyway. It only has three bedrooms, and Finn thinks we should have four. Part of me hopes the sale falls through so we can look for a larger place, but part of me is panicked because we have to be out of here and will have to figure out somewhere to go until we find something else."

"Can you put off the people moving into this house?"

"Not really," Siobhan answered. "The couple is moving here from the East Coast. I'd hate to mess them up. We're thinking about just putting our stuff into storage and seeing if we can stay with Maggie for a while."

Our Aunt Maggie lived in the main house on the property where I had my little cabin on the beach. "I'm sure she'd love to have you. Mom and Cassie are there while the condo is being worked on and Danny is there for the winter, but Maggie has a ton of guest rooms."

"She's always said we're welcome to stay there whenever we need to. I have to get back to packing, but I can pass a message on to Finn when he gets back if you want to fill me in."

I explained to Siobhan, who also happened to be the mayor of Madrona Island, that there was a new man in town intent on kicking a group of homeless people out onto the street with almost no notice. She of course was appalled, especially when she heard one of the squatters might be pregnant. Being pregnant herself, she was extra sensitive to the needs of women in the same condition.

"I understand he needs to have the building vacated to renovate. And I understand it's his building and he has the right to expect he can do with it as he pleases. But to kick a bunch of people out into the snow so close to Christmas seems heartless."

"I agree," I said. "I overheard him on the phone and it sounded like he was willing to resort to any means necessary to get the people out. I don't know for a fact that he'd use violence, but that was the vibe I was picking up. Cody and I are going over to the warehouse tomorrow morning to see exactly what the situation is and how many people will be displaced."

"That sounds like a good idea. I'll fill Finn in when he gets home. I'm not saying squatters don't need to be moved, but let's see if we can find them an alternative place to wait out the winter."

I hung up with Siobhan and tossed a log on the fire, then put the soup in a pan to heat. I defrosted the bread in the microwave and popped it into the oven to brown. The lights on the tree Cody and I had decorated reflected off the snowy window, giving the entire cabin a warm, cozy feeling. I'd just turned on some carols when Cody pulled into the drive. I hoped he'd be able to stay over tonight, but he didn't like to leave Mr. Parsons alone more often than he needed to. At some point we were going to have to discuss living arrangements after we married, but for now we were taking it slow and letting things develop naturally.

"Is Mr. Parsons okay?" I asked as Cody entered through the side door.

"He's watching old movies with Francine." Francine Rivers owned a third of the peninsula where Cody and I resided. When the founding fathers of the island divided it up, one section went to Francine's family, one to Mr. Parsons's, and the last to the Harts. Aunt Maggie lived in the big house on the property, and I lived in the summer cabin, which was right on the water and perfect for just me. Once Cody and I were married I'd probably need to move into Mr. Parsons's house with him.

"Can you stay over?" I asked.

Cody nodded. "I'll check on Mr. Parsons in the morning before we head over to the warehouse. Did you get hold of Finn?"

"He's out on a call, but I spoke to Siobhan and she'll fill him in when he gets home."

"Great. Let's eat. I'm starving."

We settled in with our soup and hot bread in front of the crackling fire. We didn't get a lot of snow on

Madrona Island, but every year I found myself wishing for Christmas snow. We'd been lucky and had had December snow several years in a row. It really added to the Christmassy feel I'd learned to embrace when I was a child.

"Did you ever find out what was going on with your mom's condo?" Cody asked.

"She said the pipes are shot and they need to completely replumb the whole place. She has to be out for a month, so she and Cassie have moved in with Maggie for the time being."

"Wow, that's tough."

I shrugged. "I guess. I don't think Maggie minds, despite the fact that Danny has moved in for the winter and now it seems Finn and Siobhan need a place to stay as well."

"I thought they were moving into their new house."

"It looks like it might fall out of escrow and their house is ready to close. It'll be a bit crowded, but Maggie's house is big, and she never minds having the various members of the Hart family staying with her when they need to."

It really did seem the entire Hart clan, other than my oldest brother, Aiden, had lived with Maggie at one time or another. Danny owned a whale-watch boat he lived on, but every now and again he leased it out for the winter and bunked with Maggie to save money during the off-season. Siobhan had lived with Maggie after returning to Madrona Island from Seattle, and I lived with her in the big house before we renovated the cabin. This was the second time my mom and my youngest sister, Cassie, had stayed with Maggie in recent years, and I imagined it wouldn't be the last. I was just finishing my soup when my phone rang. It was Siobhan.

"Did you talk to Finn?"

"Finn isn't back yet. He's at the hospital."

My heart skipped a beat. "Is he hurt?"

"He's with Aiden. Aiden was involved in the accident Finn responded to."

I put my hand to my mouth, fighting back panic. "Is he—?"

"He's going to be okay. He was driving home from the north shore and hit a patch of ice. His car slid off the road and rolled twice, but the airbag deployed and he was buckled in, so he wasn't seriously injured. Finn said not to come down. They have him sedated and he's resting. Finn's going to get all the details from the doctor and he'll fill us in when he sees us."

"Cody and I will come over to your place."

"No, don't come here, go to Maggie's. Mom, Cassie, and Danny are already there. I'm heading over as well. Finn said he'd meet us there."

When we arrived at Maggie's, the others were all sitting around discussing the situation. "Have you heard anything?" Mom asked as soon as we walked in.

"No. I just spoke to Siobhan and she said to come here. Finn will be joining us as soon as he's able to."

"I know Siobhan said to stay put, but I feel like we should be at the hospital," Danny said.

"There isn't anything we can do. Finn said Aiden is sedated and resting comfortably. With the weather the way it is, waiting really is the best choice."

The room fell silent. I understood that. We didn't know anything, so we couldn't talk about what had happened, and it seemed sort of strange to make chitchat. I hoped Siobhan got here soon. Of all the Harts, she seemed to be the best at knowing exactly what to say. Fortunately, we didn't have long to wait; she arrived shortly after Cody and I did.

"I spoke to Finn again," she began. "Aiden's going to be fine. His car is pretty much totaled, but he managed to come away with nothing more serious than a broken leg and a sprained wrist."

"So nothing life threatening?" Mom asked.

"Nothing life threatening," Siobhan confirmed. "Finn said Aiden will be released tomorrow, as long as he has somewhere to go where he can get help."

"He'll come here," Maggie spoke up. "I have plenty of room, and there will be lots of folks to help out."

"I thought you'd feel that way and so did Finn, so he arranged to have the hospital call him when Aiden's ready to be released. He'll pick him up and bring him here."

I could feel the tension in the room dissipate as everyone began to discuss which room to put Aiden in. We all agreed it should be one of the rooms on the first floor with its own bath. I had a feeling poor Aiden was going to be mothered to death with Mom and Maggie both here, but he'd been on his own for a while now, so perhaps he wouldn't mind.

Chapter 2

Thursday, December 14

When Cody and I arrived at the warehouse we found twelve people living inside. My heart ached for these people who had been forced to live in such a cold and dismal place. The group had built a small fire in the center and set up individual sleeping areas around it. The space was somewhat stuffy, but there were air vents along the roofline that took care of most of the smoke.

We explained we weren't there to hassle them but to help them find alternate housing because the new owner was going to kick them out. I could see by the looks on their faces that they were leery of us, but they seemed willing to listen, so Cody began to outline a plan to help everyone relocate and, hopefully, get a new start in life.

Two of the men, who both appeared middle-aged and street-worn, said they didn't need help from anyone, although they wouldn't mind a few bucks to see them through. It seemed obvious they'd lived on the streets for a long time and did so by choice, so Cody gave them each forty dollars. Once they had what I suspected would be drinking money, they gathered their things and headed out.

Which left ten.

"You know they're just going to convert that cash into alcohol," one of the women pointed out.

"I suspect they will," Cody answered. "But the cash was a gift, and how they use it is up to them. How about you? What's your situation?"

She looked hesitant but finally answered. "I lost my job a few months ago and couldn't pay my rent, so I got kicked out. I've been looking, but there are no jobs on the island. I'm a hard worker who's used to taking care of myself. I don't need a handout; I need a job. What I really need is for someone to look past the stringy hair and dirty clothes and take a chance on me."

Cody took out a notepad and pen. "Sounds reasonable. What's your name?"

"Isabelle," the dark-haired, dark-eyed woman answered.

"Okay, Isabelle, if I could find you a job and housing somewhere other than Madrona Island, would you take it?"

"I would."

Cody looked directly at her, as if trying to size her up and form his own opinion. "Can you give me an idea of the sort of jobs you're qualified for?"

Isabelle crossed her arms over her chest. "I've waited tables in the past. I'm a good cook and I'm good with kids. I'd love to work in a child care center, but there's no way anyone is going to let someone like me around a bunch of kids."

"Do you have a criminal record?"

Isabelle shook her head. "Not so much as a parking ticket. And I don't drink or do drugs. I just had a run of bad luck."

Cody smiled and gave her one of the vouchers we'd arranged for prior to arriving at the warehouse. "Give me a couple of days to see what I can find for you. In the meantime, I've rented you a room at the Madrona Motor Inn through the weekend. If you're willing to hang out there for a few days, I think I can come through with a job and temporary housing."

Her entire face lit up. "Really? That's great. I haven't had a shower in a month. Thank you so much."

"Cait and I are more than happy to help." Cody turned and glanced at Danny, who'd brought his truck and come to help us. "Danny will give you a ride to the motor inn, if you want to get your stuff together. The motor inn has a laundromat, and I've arranged for you to be supplied with tokens for the machines."

"Thank you again. You're so kind."

Isabelle followed Danny out to his truck, which left nine.

"How about us?" asked a man who looked like he'd lost his last drop of hope. "Me, my wife, and our four kids, have been on the street since the fishing tours shut down for the winter. We need a new start and would be willing to relocate."

Cody turned to him. "Like I said to Isabelle, I'll need a few days, but if you don't mind squeezing the family into a room with two queen beds plus a portable bed for a few days, I have a room at the motor inn for you as well. What's your name?"

"Sam."

"Okay, Sam. Tell me a bit about yourself."

"I came to the island to work on a fishing charter. My youngest has been sick, so even though I made okay money we weren't able to put anything away for the off-season. We got behind on our rent and the landlord told me he had to find a tenant who could pay. I've been looking for a job, but there hasn't been anything I'm qualified to do right now."

"And what are you qualified for?" Cody asked.

"Other than the fishing boat, I've worked construction and padded my income with some handyman work. I've worked in a warehouse and as a dishwasher. I can work a forklift and will work any hours."

Cody handed Sam a voucher. "I'll see what I can do. Get your stuff together and I'll have Danny take you over to the motor inn as soon as he gets back from dropping off Isabelle."

And then there were three.

"So, what's your story?" Cody asked a kid who looked to be no older than eighteen or nineteen.

At first I thought he was going to refuse to answer. He seemed to have a chip on his shoulder, and I wasn't certain he'd be open to Cody's brand of disciplined and organized help. I half-expected him to say something rude and leave, but instead he began to speak. "My name is Bobby. I got into some trouble and my parents kicked me out. Got a temp job on a fishing boat that traveled between here and Alaska, but the job's over, so here I am."

"How did you like working on the fishing boat?" Cody asked him.

The kid shrugged. "It was okay but not really my thing. What I'd really like to do is head down to San Francisco. I feel like I would fit in there, if you know what I mean."

"Would you have a place to stay once you got there?"

"I have a cousin who might let me crash with him for a few days until I could get a job."

Cody handed the boy a voucher. "I'll see what I can do about transportation. I'll need a day or two, so if you're willing to be patient, there's a room for you at the motor inn as well."

"The place seems like a dump, but it's better than here. Thanks, man, you're okay."

Cody turned to the old man and pregnant woman, who were the two left. He waited, but neither spoke up, so he got the ball rolling, addressing the old man first. The poor guy was thin and pale and looked to be at least seventy.

"What's your name?" Cody asked.

"Burt, and I don't need your charity."

"That's fine." Cody paused and waited for the man to let down his guard just a bit before he continued. "I understand why you might prefer to handle things on your own. Have you lived on the island long?"

"Long enough to know I don't want to move to some dang blasted city."

"Understood. Do you have family who can help you out?"

"Nope. It's just me. I know you're here to get us all out so the new owner can tear this place down, but I've been taking care of myself for a whole lot of years and I don't need some do-good whippersnapper taking care of me now.'

"I can appreciate that," Cody responded. "Would you be interested in a job?"

"Job?"

"How are you with dogs?"

"Dogs?"

"I live with a man, Mr. Parsons. He's about your age, but he has some medical issues and has a hard time getting around in the snow. He has a dog, Rambler. When the weather is bad I help him out by walking the dog and making sure he gets the exercise he needs. The thing is, I've been real busy lately and could use some help. I can't pay you a lot, but the job includes room and board."

"You sure this isn't some thinly veiled attempt at charity?"

"Not at all. I really do need someone to walk Rambler and Mr. Parsons really could use someone to check in on him now and then. How about it?"

Burt nodded his head. "Okay. If you're sure this is a real job I guess I might be able to help you out."

And then there was one.

Cody turned his attention to the young woman, who looked to be five or six months along. I'd been watching her since we arrived and given the look of distrust, fear, and suspicion on her face, I suspected she could be the hardest sell of all.

"Do you like books?" I asked the girl before Cody could even get started.

"Books?"

"I co-own a bookstore with my best friend, Tara O'Brian. We sell books and coffee and also have a cat lounge, where customers can hang out with the cats while they read. We're always busy at this time of year. Totally swamped, in fact. We've been looking for some part-time help, but so far we haven't had much luck finding anyone who's interested in temporary work. I don't know you, but you seem confident and independent. I think you might be perfect, if you're interested."

The girl frowned, but I could tell she was considering it.

"Tara has an extra bedroom," I added. "In the past she's offered it to our temporary help. I'm sure she'd be willing to let you stay there if you wanted to."

"I have business on the island. I'm not sure I can make a full-time commitment."

"Part time would be perfect. Please consider it. We really could use the help."

"Can I see the place before I decide?"

"Absolutely. In fact, if you want I can take you over there now, while Cody and Danny are getting the others settled."

"Okay. Just give me a minute to get my things."

And then there were none.

******

I hoped Tara really wouldn't mind both hiring and housing the young woman, whose name, I learned, was Willow. I didn't know a lot about her—she'd refused to provide even a last name at this point—but she didn't seem like a serial killer, and Tara had always had a soft spot for expectant mothers in need.

I quickly texted her and explained the situation while Willow gathered her things, so Tara wasn't totally shocked when we arrived, and explained why I'd brought her to the store.

"I'm very happy to meet you," Tara greeted Willow.

Willow's expression softened as she looked around. "Wow; this place is real nice. Are the cats here all the time?"

"Every day we're open," Tara answered, as she slipped the books she was stocking onto a shelf. "You aren't allergic, are you?"

"No. I'm not allergic. I love cats. We always had a couple in the house when I was growing up."

"Fantastic," Tara responded. "So, about the job? Cait and I need any help we can get right now, but it would be good to know a bit about you, so we can best utilize your skills. Have you ever worked in retail?"

"I have. And I love to read. Or at least I used to, when I could afford to buy books. It's been a while."

"That's' fine. We need all kinds of help at this time of the year. The inventory seems to fly off the shelves as soon as we can stock it and we always have a line out the door for the coffee bar when the ferry comes in."

"I don't know how to make all those fancy coffee drinks," Willow admitted.

"We can work around that." Tara smiled. "I could use someone to ring up purchases as I process orders. Does it seem like Coffee Cat Books might be a place you'd be interested in working?"

"I would. It's lovely here. Although…" Willow looked down at her clothes. "I don't have anything nice enough to wear to work at a place like this."

"You look like you're about the same size as my sister Siobhan," I offered. "She's pregnant as well, so I know she has some appropriate clothing. She loves to do makeovers, and I'm sure she'd be happy to lend you something until you get your first check and can buy something more to your liking."

Willow didn't answer, but I could tell by the look on her face she was intrigued by our offer, but one wrong word might send her taking off. I noticed a look of longing on her face, but it also appeared she was scared and somewhat leery about everything that was happening. I guess I could understand that. I wondered what had gone on in her life to bring her to this moment in time.

"How about if I call Siobhan to see if she has time to pop over?" I added, attempting to restart the conversation. "She works close by, so it shouldn't be a problem. You'll like her. I promise."

Luckily, Siobhan was in her office and wasn't overly busy, so she agreed to stop by the store. Willow reminded me a lot of Siobhan, at least in terms of looks. Both were blond and beautiful, and I could see the moment my sister arrived that she was going to be a huge influence on the young girl, who seemed as enchanted with my friendly, outgoing sister as everyone who met her always seemed to be.

"Well, aren't you simply beautiful?" Siobhan said after giving Willow an unscripted yet welcoming hug. "And those highlights." Siobhan touched her hair. "Are they natural?"

"Everything you see is natural," Willow answered. "I haven't had money for spa treatments lately."

"Willow is thinking about helping us at the store," Tara interrupted. "She'll need some clothes. Can you help her out?"

"Absolutely," Siobhan answered. "I have a couple of outfits I never wear that would be perfect for her. We'll need to go grab them before Finn takes the boxes to the storage unit we rented." Siobhan looked at Willow. "Can you come with me now?"

Willow looked at Tara.

"I think now would be perfect," Tara responded. "Willow will be staying with me for the time being. Maybe you can take her by my condo and get her comfortable in the spare bedroom when you're done."

"I'd be happy to." Siobhan looped her arm through Willow's. "Come along now; we're going to have the best time today."

It did my heart good to see a lightness in Willow's step as she allowed herself to be dragged along by my assertive, enthusiastic sister.

"Thanks for going along with my plan," I said after they left.

"I'm happy to. That poor girl. Do you know anything about her situation?"

I shook my head. "No. Only that she was living with the others in the warehouse. I could see she wasn't going to take a handout, but I sensed she might be willing to take a job, so I asked her before I had the opportunity to speak to you about it. She looks so young. I can't imagine being homeless and pregnant and completely on my own."

"You did the right thing bringing her here. Maybe she'll open up to us once she gets to know us a bit."

"That's what I'm hoping, but we need to be careful not to push. I think she has more potential to clam up than open up at this point."

"I agree. We'll take it slow. By the way, how's Aiden?" Tara asked.

"Finn said he's banged up a bit but will be fine. He's taking him over to Maggie's this afternoon. The whole gang has gathered there for one reason or another, so he'll have lots of caregivers to see to his every need."

Tara laughed. "Poor guy. I hope he's up for all that caregiving."

"Aiden's tough. He'll get through it. I'm just happy he's able to come home for everyone to baby."

"Yeah. It could have been worse." Tara picked up a cute Santa decoration. "I meant to tell you, Alex stopped by earlier."

"Alex Turner?" Tara had referred to the young man who'd worked for us as Santa two years earlier. Not only was he an excellent Santa but after a whole lot of sleuthing we'd found out he was the man we'd been looking for at the time.

"Yep. He'll be on the island until after New Year's. Apparently, he's been in Europe since graduating college last spring, but he figured it was time to come home and start thinking about his career."

"I'm sorry I missed him. I'll have to make a point of going out to the house to see him. Was he alone?" The last time Alex had visited the island he'd brought along a group of friends who'd gotten him into a whole lot of trouble.

"He was, although he said he had plans to get together with Balthazar."

"I'm sure he'll enjoy seeing him."

"Are you still planning to head over to Balthazar's island today?" Tara asked.

"Yes. I'm going to take Ebenezer back, and I want to ask him about jobs and housing. Two of the twelve people Cody and I met with were happy to receive a monetary donation and went on their way. Another wanted to go to San Francisco. Cody's planning to confirm that he has a place to stay; if he does, Danny's going to take him to Seattle and buy him an airline ticket. Willow's safe with us for the time being, and an older gentleman will be staying with Mr. Parsons for a while. That still leaves a woman who really wants a job and is willing to relocate and a man with a wife and four children. I'm hoping I can talk Balthazar into providing all of them with jobs and places to live."

"Does Balthazar still own businesses on the island?"

"No, but he does in Seattle, and these people are willing to relocate."

"I have to hand it to you," Tara said. "You set out to find alternative housing for the people living in the warehouse and you did just that."

"Cody came up with the plan, and it did seem to go really well. I feel like it was almost too easy, though. I keep waiting for the other shoe to drop."

Chapter 3

Getting to Balthazar's island required a ferry ride to San Juan Island and then a water taxi out to his estate. As I mentioned, I'd first met him two Christmases ago, when he was the one threatening to kick people out into the snow just days before Christmas. I'd traveled to the island to try to talk him out of the evictions and ended up making a deal with him that required me to find his son, who had been kidnapped as an infant and was presently in his twenties. As it turned out, the man I was looking for was Alex Turner. It hadn't been easy, but I'd succeeded in reuniting the pair, both of whom came out of the experience changed men.

I felt good about the role I'd played in reuniting Balthazar and Alex, but I hoped finding solutions to our current needs would be quite a bit easier. Between the Christmas play, the upcoming holiday, our Christmas Eve dinner, and now Aiden's car accident,

I felt like I already had a lot on my mind without adding a complicated mystery.

The ferry ride to San Juan Island was accomplished in short order. Ebenezer and I hurried to the marina to catch the water taxi I'd booked. It was a lot smaller than the ferry, so the ride over to the island on a snowy day was a bit rougher and a whole lot colder, despite the thin cover that had been pulled over the passenger area. It could have been a miserable ride, but the cat and I cuddled under a blanket that made it tolerable. Once we entered the calmer water on the backside of the chain of islands, the wind died down and the ride became almost pleasant.

"Here we are, ma'am," the driver said as he pulled up to the dock. "Would you like me to wait?"

"Yes, please. I won't be long." I grabbed Ebenezer and started up the snowy path from the dock to the house.

The first time I'd come to Balthazar's island the gate between the dock and the house had been locked and I'd had to find another way in, but ever since we'd become friends Balthazar had begun leaving the gate open on the chance I might stop by.

I climbed the steps to the front door, knocked, and waited. The wind had intensified a bit and I had a feeling the taxi ride back to San Juan Island was going to be even bumpier than it had been on the way here. I wasn't looking forward to the icy ride back without the cat to cuddle with, but I was happy I'd had the chance to reunite Balthazar with his best friend.

"Cait," Balthazar greeted me, a look of surprise on his thin, weathered face. "I wasn't expecting you today."

"I'm here to return Ebenezer." I smiled at the old man, who was gnarled and stooped with age, then nodded to the cat in my arms.

Balthazar stepped aside to reveal a cat identical to the one I was holding standing behind him.

"Ebenezer?" I said in surprise.

"He hasn't left the island for months," Balthazar confirmed as he tiled his head of white hair and waved me forward. "Do come in. It's chilly out today and I have a fire going in the study."

I followed Balthazar and Ebenezer down the dark, narrow hallway, wondering the entire time how it was I was holding a cat identical in every way to the one I was following. I felt like I'd landed in some sort of a time loop, or perhaps a multidimensional situation in which two beings that were exactly the same could exist at the same time. One thing was certain: a visit to Tansy, the woman who served as something of a guardian for the magical cats who often appeared on Madrona Island, was going to be the very next thing I did.

"I'm sorry you wasted time coming out to bring home a cat who was already here, but I'm happy to see you," Balthazar said, after indicating I should take a seat near the fire. Although Balthazar was a very wealthy man, he chose to live very frugally, closing off most of his mansion and living in only a handful of rooms on the first floor. The study was where he could be found most of the time. "Can you stay and read to me?"

"I have a taxi waiting, so I'll need to come back to read to you. I had another reason for coming today, however, so it wasn't a wasted trip." I looked at the cats again. "I know what I'm seeing, but I'm still having a hard time believing these are different cats." I set the animal in my arms on the floor next to Ebenezer. Even sitting side by side, the cats appeared to be exactly the same. "Did Ebenezer ever sire kittens?" If the cat I'd found at St. Patrick's was one of Ebenezer's offspring that could account for the fact that the two were so much alike.

"Not that I'm aware of. Ebenezer had been altered before I found him, but I don't know what he may have done prior to coming to live with me. The similarity really is remarkable. Where did you find this cat?"

"He found me, at St. Pat's. I really thought it was Ebenezer, come to help with the warehouse situation."

"There's a warehouse situation?" Balthazar asked.

I explained about the new man in town and his intention to kick out the squatters living in the warehouse, the temporary solution Cody and I had come up with, and our need of both jobs and housing for Isabelle and Sam. Balthazar informed me that he'd turned over the day-to-day running of the businesses and rental properties he owned to a manager, but he promised to check with him to see if there was something they could work out.

"Tara told me Alex had been by the bookstore this morning," I said.

"He must have arrived early. When I last spoke to him, he indicated he probably wouldn't be able to get away until next week. I'm so looking forward to seeing him. I can't believe it's only been two years since I learned my son was still alive. In many ways I feel we've lived a lifetime in that time."

I smiled. It made me proud that I'd been able to help reunite father and son. "Do you think you'll make the trip to Madrona earlier now that you know Alex is there?"

"Perhaps."

"I'm sure he's anxious to see you. It would be fun to help him decorate the house for the holiday."

"I haven't had a tree in more than twenty years."

"Tara told me Alex seems to have the decorating bug this year. Oh, before I forget, I want to invite both you and Alex to the Christmas Eve dinner Cody and I are having again this year."

"I'd enjoy that. I'll speak to Alex and see what he has on his mind for the holiday."

"Great." I glanced at my watch. "The water taxi is waiting, so I should get going."

"I've enjoyed our visit despite its brevity."

"I always enjoy seeing you as well."

"I'll call you as soon as I have a chance to speak with my business manager."

"Thank you. I'd appreciate that."

The ride back to San Juan Island was cold and bumpy and not at all pleasant. I knew the ferry ride from San Juan to Madrona Island would at least be warm, so I forced myself to focus on that as the cat and I sped across the choppy water. Once we returned to Madrona Island, we headed to Herbalities, the herb and fortune-telling shop Tansy owned and ran with her roommate and partner, Bella. I figured if a cat who looked exactly like Ebenezer found me at St. Patrick's during a snowstorm shortly before

Christmas the same way Ebenezer had two years before, there was most likely a mystical reason he was here, and if another of Tansy's cats had come into my life, she'd know why. The arrival of the cats usually accompanied a death, though I hoped that wasn't the case this time.

"Cait, Marley, I've been expecting you," Tansy greeted us the minute we walked through the door of the shop. Unlike her tall, blond roommate, Tansy was petite, with long black hair that fell to her waist.

"Marley? As in Jacob Marley of Scrooge and Marley?"

"The name is the same," Tansy confirmed.

"This is going to get confusing; Marley is Aunt Maggie's best friend. How about we change it to Harley?"

"Fine with me. Is it okay with you?" Tansy asked the cat.

The cat meowed in what seemed to be agreement.

"Anyway, Marley, or I guess I should say Harley, found me last night. At the time I assumed he was Ebenezer, so I took him out to Balthazar's island to bring him home, but Ebenezer was already there. I assume you know why the cat came to me. There hasn't been a murder, has there?"

"No. Not a murder."

I let out a breath of relief. "Good. I'm happy to hear that." I looked down at the cat. "But there's a reason Harley has found me?"

Tansy nodded.

"Can you tell me what Harley and I are supposed to be doing?"

Tansy seemed to float effortlessly across the room as she crossed to stand next to me. She took the cat from my arms and looked him in the eye. Neither spoke, but I felt the two were communicating. Tansy set the cat on the floor, then turned and looked at me. "There's a girl you've met recently. She's with child."

"Yes. Her name is Willow. She was living with some other homeless people in an old warehouse that's recently been sold. Cody and I are helping to find them all alternate housing. Willow will be working for Coffee Cat Books for the time being and staying in Tara's extra room."

Tansy frowned, which wasn't an expression I normally associated with her. "The child she's carrying will be an important figure in the future. Millions of lives will be saved because of the technology he develops."

I grinned. "That's great. I'm sure Willow will be thrilled to hear it."

"You can't tell her. Ever. Life must be allowed to unfold naturally, without expectation or interference."

I hesitated. "Okay. I guess that makes sense. But why are you telling me, and why is Harley here?"

Tansy paused and closed her eyes. She began to speak without opening them. "I sense the fabric of time is in a fragile state. The baby's path is shrouded in uncertainty." Tansy opened her eyes. "It's my feeling there are multiple life paths the child can travel, but only one will lead him to his intended destiny. The cat is here to help assure that the baby ends up on the right path."

Color me confused. Perhaps I was dreaming, because despite everything I'd experienced in the past few years, this whole cat-from-the-future thing was just too much.

"Okay, wait. First you make it sound as if I can't do anything to alter the natural course of events and then you make it sound as if it's my responsibility to ensure that Willow's baby ends up on the right life path. Which is it?"

I felt tension in my body as I watched Tansy struggle for the answer. In all the time I'd known her, she'd always seemed to know the answers, even if she didn't always choose to share them. The fact that she seemed to be as confused now as I was didn't lend itself to a feeling of confidence on my part.

"Tansy?" I asked again.

"I think we need to be careful with this one," she finally said. "I'm afraid I'm not getting a clear reading. What I do know is that Willow's baby will be a genius, and his natural intelligence combined with a first-rate education will allow him to start a company in which a technology will be developed that will save millions of lives. If he ends up on the wrong path he may not have the education and opportunities he needs to do that." Tansy paused once again, then looked at me. "Tell me about this young woman who carries the child."

"I don't know much about her at all," I admitted. "I found her living with other homeless people in a warehouse. She appears to be alone on the island. She told me her first name but little else. I do know she has a reason for being here. She told us she would only be available to work part time because she needed the rest of the time to do whatever she came here for."

Tansy folded her arms across her chest. "Let's start there. See if you can get her to open up to you.

Perhaps her reason for being on the island has something to do with the crossroads I sense."

I picked Harley up off the floor. "I'll see what I can do. Let me know if you come up with anything more specific."

"I will, and godspeed."

Harley and I left Herbalities and headed to the newspaper to chat with Cody. Suddenly, my already complicated life had become a lot more so. I wasn't sure how I was going to juggle everything on my plate, but it all seemed pretty important, so I'd simply have to get organized and do whatever it took to pull off my own Christmas miracle.

Cody was on the phone when I arrived, so I set Harley down, poured myself a cup of coffee, and sat down on one of the stools lining the counter. Harley jumped up onto the counter and began to purr as Cody caressed him behind the ears as he spoke.

"I see Ebenezer is still with us," Cody said after he hung up.

"Not Ebenezer; Harley."

Cody frowned.

"Ebenezer is and has been with Balthazar on his island for the past month at least. When I realized there were two identical cats I went to see Tansy and she told me this one is Harley. I'm not sure if he's from the future or a protector of some part of the future, but apparently, he's here to make sure Willow's child ends up on the path he's destined to follow."

Cody sat down on a stool on the other side of the counter. "Huh?"

"That's what I said. This thing is a bit too sci-fi for my taste, but apparently, Willow and her child are at an important crossroads, and outcomes and decisions matter."

"Tansy told you Harley was from the future?" Cody clarified.

"No. She couldn't seem to get a clear reading. I'm a little worried about this one. Normally, I'm the one who's confused, while Tansy is confident and mysterious, but I could tell even she doesn't quite know what to make of things now. If a witch who can foretell the future isn't certain about it, I think we have a pretty complicated task ahead of us."

"Did Tansy seem sure the cat is here to help guide Willow to the right path?"

I nodded. "That was the one thing she was certain about. She doesn't have all the details, but it seems Willow's baby will be highly intelligent and will develop some sort of technology that will save millions of lives someday. Tansy didn't know why Harley was here or what our task will entail, but she seems to think it's important that we find out what Willow is on the island to accomplish."

"I do wonder how she ended up living in an abandoned warehouse with a bunch of homeless people."

"Did you and Danny get the others settled?"

"We did. Did you have any luck with Balthazar regarding housing and jobs for Sam and Isabelle?"

"He needed to check with his business manager, but my sense was that he'd work something out. He promised to get back to me in a day or two. Did you confirm that the kid who wants to go to San Francisco has a place to stay?"

Cody nodded. "I bought him an airline ticket for tomorrow. Danny's going to give him a ride to the airport. If Balthazar can come up with jobs and housing for Sam and Isabelle, we'll just need to figure out how to help Willow and Burt."

"I'm hoping Willow can tell us what she needs. Tara texted me to say she's at her place right now, and we're going to meet there when Coffee Cat Books closes, which is in," I glanced at the clock on the wall, "thirty-seven minutes. Were you able to get any additional information from Burt after I left?"

"Yes, I was. It turns out he owned a house on the island for almost twenty years. His wife became ill a couple of years ago and he was forced to take out a mortgage to pay her medical expenses. She passed away nine months ago, leaving him with a huge debt."

"The bank foreclosed?"

"Burt needed to pay for the medication his wife needed right away, and a loan from the bank was going to take too long, so he borrowed the money from Jack Forrester, a hard money lender. After his wife's death, Burt fell into a deep depression and got behind on his payments to Forrester. The house went to him, and he evicted Burt two months ago. Burt says the place is just sitting empty, so I thought I'd see if there's a way to negotiate a deal so Burt can move back in."

"You're a good guy, Cody West." I stood on tiptoe and kissed him hard on the lips. "I need to get going if I'm going to meet Tara and Willow on time, but we should make plans for this evening. I planned to go over to Maggie's when I got home to check on Aiden. If you want to meet me there we can have dinner after."

"Okay. I'll head to Maggie's when I'm done here. Hopefully, by the end of the evening we'll know enough to come up with a plan to help both Burt and Willow."

Chapter 4

When I arrived at Tara's, Willow was settled in watching television with Tara's cat, Bandit, on her lap. The minute I set Harley on the floor he ran over to where they were sitting and the two greeted each other like long-lost friends.

"Do you know this cat?" I asked Willow.

She shook her head. "No, though I feel like I should, even though I'm certain I've never seen him before. Is he your cat?"

Okay, at least now I was a bit more confident the cat really was here to help Willow.

"No, not mine exactly. His name is Harley and he's staying with me temporarily, much like you're staying with Tara."

Willow hugged him to her chest. "He's beautiful."

It was a relief to see Willow clean and comfortable in the clothes Siobhan had lent her. She looked a lot younger now that she'd had the chance to shower, and I wondered how old she actually was. "I love the outfit Siobhan helped you pick out."

"Your sister's great. She gave me a whole bag full of clothes and told me to keep them. It's been a long time since I've had anything this nice to wear, although I'm saving the best outfits for work."

"Speaking of work," I decided to jump right in, "Tara and I have a few questions we need to ask before we can get started."

I could see Willow tense. "What kind of questions?"

"Just things like your last name, social security number, birthdate. You know, the stuff all employers are supposed to gather."

Willow frowned. "I see." She hesitated. "I guess that would be okay."

I nodded at Tara to get a pad and pencil and begin making notes. I figured once I got Willow talking I'd move on to the questions I really needed to ask.

"My name is Willow Wood. My social security number is…" I listened while Willow rattled off the information we'd need to process her employment. It turned out she *was* younger than I'd first imagined. I couldn't understand how the poor thing had ended up homeless and pregnant with seemingly no one in the world to care for or worry about her. The tricky part, I realized, was going to be getting her to share why she was on the island and who the baby's father might be.

"Who should I put as your emergency contact?" Tara asked.

Willow froze. "I don't have one. It's just me."

Tara set down her pad and pen and looked toward Willow, still clinging to Harley on the sofa. "Working at Coffee Cat Books won't be dangerous by any stretch of the imagination, but we do like to have the number of someone to contact just in case. Perhaps the baby's father?"

Willow looked down at her hands. I hoped she'd volunteer the information, but she just stared down at the cat in her arms.

Finally, I decided to jump in with both feet. "Are you in some sort of trouble? Because if you are, we want to help."

"It's not that," Willow whispered.

"I know you only just met us and have no reason to trust us, but my intuition tells me there's a story behind your presence on Madrona Island. I want you to know that Tara and I are here to help you with whatever you need. We aren't here to judge or to make you do anything you don't want to. Just help. I promise."

Willow continued to pet the cat but still didn't answer.

"Harley came to me because he wants to help as well."

Willow looked up. "He came to you?"

"I didn't want to say as much before because some people find my situation odd, but I've somehow become a guardian for the island's cats. When there's a mystery to solve, one of the cats will come to me and we solve it together. I'm not sure exactly what the present mystery entails, but I do know Harley and I are supposed to help you."

Willow frowned but still didn't respond. I hoped she was at least considering what I'd said.

"You said you felt like you knew the cat. The two of you are somehow connected. He must be here to help you, and the fact that he came to me should indicate I'm here to help you as well."

"My life is complicated."

"Figured."

"I've made some mistakes. Big ones. What I want most is to make things right."

Okay, it appeared we were getting somewhere. "Does your intuition tell you to trust Harley?"

Willow nodded.

"Do you think you can trust me too?"

Willow titled her head to one side. She looked directly at me, as if studying me and trying to figure out my true intent. Tara was watching our exchange but so far had elected to let me do the talking.

"What do you want to know?" Willow finally asked.

"Why don't you start by telling us what brought you to the island?" I suggested.

"It's a long story."

I sat down on the sofa next to Willow. "I have time."

Willow set Harley down before standing up. She began to pace. I waited until she eventually began to speak.

"My life was normal until four years ago. I lived in an upper-middle-class household, went to a private school with an accelerated curriculum, and had friends. I was on the fast track to an Ivy League college and a fabulous career, and then my parents were killed in a small plane accident."

I wanted to say how sorry I was but decided not to interrupt.

"My mother's sister became my legal guardian. I didn't know her all that well because she and my mother hadn't been close, but I hoped for the best. That wasn't to be, however. It became evident to me after only two days that Aunt Stacy was more interested in spending the money my parents had left to provide for me than in taking care of me, so I ran away. I was just sixteen then, but I knew I was better off on my own."

Willow paused, but still I waited.

"I did okay for a while. I never did find a place where I felt I could settle, so I moved around a lot, taking odd jobs along the way. Eventually, I ended up in Seattle, where I got a job in a back-alley bar. I'm still not twenty-one, so I was never officially hired, but it didn't seem to matter. As far as jobs go it wasn't great, but I'd had worse. I worked for tips and some weeks were better than others, so I mostly lived on the street. I probably would have moved on by now, but last summer I met Trace. At least I think his name was Trace. He made a comment about the name fitting his lifestyle because he would roll into a town, stay for a while, and then disappear without a trace."

"So Trace might have been a nickname," I said.

Willow shrugged. "I suppose. I didn't ask and, to be honest, at the time it didn't matter. What we had was brief and simple. He was sitting on a park bench playing his guitar and I was out for an evening stroll. I paused to listen to the music and we started talking. One thing led to another and four weeks after he left Seattle I realized I was pregnant. I knew he was just passing through and had no intention of fathering a child and my own life was such a mess that I decided to put the baby up for adoption. I know there are a lot of great couples out there looking for babies, so I took my time searching for the perfect parents for my child. I wanted someone who could provide him with the lifestyle I'd once enjoyed."

"And did you find someone?" I asked.

Willow nodded. "I found a wonderful couple. They're both professionals who seem completely devoted to each other. They spent their youth focusing on their careers and never took the time to have a child, but now that they were in their forties they realized they wanted a baby more than anything. They were quite well off and assured me that my baby would go to the best schools and have the opportunities only available to children from families with means."

"It sounds like you found awesome parents for your baby. I know giving him up will be hard, but I think you have a solid plan."

"I do. There's only one problem. The couple wants the baby's father to sign off on the adoption so there won't be any problems with custody in the future."

"And you don't know where he is," I realized.

Willow took a deep breath and let it out slowly. "Exactly. Trace said he was on his way to Madrona Island to work on a fishing boat for the summer. I came here almost six weeks ago to find him. I've picked up a few leads, but they've gone cold. I'm out of money and running out of time and I should probably accept defeat, but I really want my baby to have the life the Plimptons can provide. I keep thinking I'll catch a break eventually and figure out where Trace went from here if he's already moved on."

Suddenly it all made sense. Harley and I were here to help Willow find the father of her child so he could be adopted into a family that would provide him with the education and financial means he'd need to someday start his company. "Do you have a photo of the man who fathered your child?"

"No. I didn't have a camera or a phone."

"If our task is to find this man—and I now believe it is—it will help to have a picture. Tara is an excellent artist. Do you think you could describe Trace to her? If we can get a good enough likeness it will help us when we talk to people who might have come into contact with him."

Willow shrugged. "I can try."

"And we'll need to know everything you've already tried. Every person you've spoken to and every business you've visited."

"Are you sure you want to help me? It's beginning to seem pointless."

"We're sure," I said with conviction.

******

Later that evening, the entire Hart family gathered at Maggie's for a meal and to fuss over Aiden. Although he was pretty banged up and it was hard to see my oldest brother in pain, I was so happy he hadn't sustained much more severe injuries that I was enjoying the others, sharing the festive meal Mom and Maggie had prepared.

In addition to Cody, Finn, and the entire Hart clan, Father Kilian had joined us as well. I had a feeling the next phase of the plan he and Aunt Maggie had come up with to be together after all these years was about to begin if their shy glances and secretive smiles were any indication.

"As long as we're all here, I'd like us to discuss everyone's plans for Christmas," Mom announced as we devoured the delicious food.

"Cody and I have the candle ceremony in the town square this Saturday, the Christmas play at the church on Saturday of next week, and the Christmas Eve party at Mr. Parsons's, to which you're all invited, on Sunday," I started. "I guess I figured we'd be having Christmas dinner here?"

"I'm planning on it," Maggie confirmed. "In fact, I thought maybe I'd do brunch for everyone gathered here tonight and invite a few others for dinner: Tara, Parker, and Amy; Sister Mary; Gabe; and Marley."

I couldn't help but giggle at Maggie's reference to her best friend and business partner, Marley Donnelly. It really was a good thing we'd decided to change the cat's name to Harley.

"Is something funny?" Maggie asked.

"No. It's just that the new cat who's staying with me was named Marley before I changed it to Harley. It hit me how really confusing that would be."

"You have a new cat?" Mom asked. "Has someone died?"

I shook my head. "No, no one's died. It seems the cat is here to help out with the relocation of the homeless people who were living in the warehouse." I decided not to be more specific; Tansy had indicated it was going to be a delicate dance, walking the line between aiding the future and interfering with it, so I figured the fewer people who knew what was going on, the better.

"That's good," Mom responded. "Murder at Christmas is so unseemly."

I wanted to say that murder at any time was unseemly but held my tongue. Cassie helped by asking to invite the boy she'd been dating to dinner. I expected our mother to say no, but she said inviting him was an excellent idea because she'd been wanting to meet the young man her youngest daughter had been spending an inordinate amount of time with.

"Finn and I plan to attend the play at the church, spend Christmas Eve at Mr. Parsons's, and Christmas Day with the family, but we have a formal dinner this Saturday, so we'll miss the candle ceremony."

"Miss the candle ceremony?" I asked. "But you're the mayor!"

"I know. And I'm extremely conflicted. But the sheriff invited all the resident deputies and their wives to dinner on San Juan Island on Saturday and Finn and I feel like we need to attend."

"I think you've made the right choice," Maggie offered. "We'll of course miss you both, but the community found between co-workers is as important as any."

"I'm going to skip the candle ceremony too," Danny chimed in. "I wish I could say I had a good reason, but the truth is, I have a date."

Aiden pointed at his foot. "I'm out as well."

Mom looked at Cassie, who grimaced. "I have plans too. I didn't want to bring it up, but with everyone else bailing I'd like to go to the party my friends are throwing."

Mom sighed. "Oh, very well. It will just be a small group representing the Hart family this year."

After dinner Cody and I went back to my cabin. It was nice having the whole family together, but I was looking forward to some quiet time as well. The snow had stopped, so we bundled up and took a walk along the moonlit beach. Max ran on ahead of us as Cody and I walked hand in hand.

"I can't believe I only have ten days to finish my shopping, wrap my gifts, do some baking, and get everything ready for the party on the twenty-fourth." It suddenly hit me just how much I still had to do.

"Let me help," Cody offered.

"You have a lot to do yourself."

"We're a team," Cody reminded me. "If we're committed to tackling life together we can certainly tackle Christmas."

I smiled. "You're right. We're a team. The point is how to juggle everything *and* help Burt get his house back *and* find the man who fathered Willow's baby."

"When we get back to the cabin we'll come up with a plan to tackle both the daddy hunt and Burt's problem. As for Christmas, how about we go shopping after we both get off tomorrow? We can grab dinner in town, then come back here and have a wrapping party."

I leaned my head on Cody's shoulder. "That sounds good. Being organized will be the key to getting everything done. Did you remember to call about renting extra tables and chairs for the party?"

"It's all taken care of. I went ahead and rented tablecloths, dishes, and serving trays as well. How's the food coming along?"

"Francine is organizing the food," I informed Cody.

He squeezed my hand. "See? We're crushing this thing."

"Yeah, I guess we are. I haven't sent formal invitations, but I've spoken to everyone we discussed inviting them personally. I figure there'll be guests who show up at the last minute, so I think we should add at least fifteen percent to whatever head count we come up with. So far we're at fifty-seven."

Cody laughed. "Do you remember that first year, when we were going to have a small dinner with Mr. Parsons so he wouldn't be alone at Christmas?"

"It was a sweet idea that quickly took on a life of its own, but we managed to bring Christmas to a lot of people who would have been alone otherwise, and Mr. Parsons is a changed man because of that first party. It's a lot of work, but it's important as well."

"Yes, and I love that our first tradition as a couple is one that brings happiness to so many of our friends and neighbors."

I smiled. "As traditions go, a party for those who have nowhere else to go is pretty awesome. Maybe it's something our children and even our grandchildren will carry on to benefit the community."

"I love that thought."

"It's nice to think about a tradition we started living on into the future." I stopped walking and looked up at the cloud-covered sky. "But first things first. How about we head back and open a bottle of wine? We can make a list of ways to tackle the missing daddy situation and then maybe we could start practicing for our honeymoon."

"Practicing?"

"You know what they say: Practice makes perfect, and I want our honeymoon to be the most perfect ever."

Cody stopped walking. He turned me in his arms so we were facing each other. He leaned his head down and kissed me in a way that I felt our souls meld. "Perhaps we should skip the list-making and get right to the practicing."

"Yeah," I gasped as his cold lips found my throat. "Maybe we should."

Chapter 5

Friday, December 15

I came downstairs the next morning to find Cody chatting with Harley. I paused to listen to what was being said because, while Cody completely supported the cats who came into our lives, he hadn't ever sat down and chatted with them before. Harley was on the kitchen table while Cody sipped a cup of coffee with a piece of paper in front of him.

"The odds that the man who fathered Willow's baby is still on the island are slim," Cody said. "I hope you have a better plan in mind than swatting my pen out of my hand and onto the floor every time I try to make a note."

"Meow."

"Yeah. I didn't think so. I meant to ask Cait last night if she'd asked Willow about the leads she'd already followed up on. I'd ask her now, but it seems the princess is still in bed."

Princess? Oh, he was in big trouble. I was about to say something to defend my late morning when Harley jumped off the table and headed up the stairs. Cody turned and saw me standing at the top.

"I guess you heard that?"

"I guess I did."

"Sorry," he said sheepishly. "I know you aren't fond of the princess nickname. I was just anxious for you to get up. It's nine-twenty."

"Someone," I said as I started down the stairs, "I won't say who, kept me up much later than I'm accustomed to."

Cody grinned. "You did say practice makes perfect."

I grinned back. "Yeah, I guess I did at that." I paused to pour myself a cup of coffee. "What smells so good?"

"Bacon and egg casserole. I have it warming in the oven. Grab a seat and I'll cut you a slice."

I took a long sip of my hot coffee as I settled onto the chair Cody had just vacated. I could have taken the one across the table, but he'd already warmed this one up, and having to warm up the second chair could be his punishment for the princess comment.

"So, did you happen to ask Willow about the leads she'd already followed up on?" Cody asked after setting the plate of egg casserole in front of me.

"I did," I answered after taking my first bite. "Basically, she said her plan when she came to Madrona Island was to visit fishing charter operations to ask about Trace. At first no one admitted to knowing who he was, but then she met a whale-watch captain who said someone fitting her description had worked for a company in the area. The captain said he called himself Tim, not Trace, so he couldn't be certain it was the same person. Willow asked around, trying to find the man Trace might have worked for, but she was told he'd left the island."

"So she hit a dead end."

"Mostly. However, while she was looking for him, she picked up another lead. She was told Tim had been seen drinking in a local bar with Wilton Palmer. Palmer runs a long-haul cargo operation out of Seattle."

"Cargo? As in shipping containers?"

"Exactly. Willow tracked Palmer down and was told he knew Tim, but he hadn't worked for him. Palmer told her he'd taken a job on a fishing boat out of Seward, Alaska. It took Willow a while, but eventually she met a man who operated an air cargo service who let her tag along on his next trip north. When she arrived in Seward she asked around but came up empty, so she came back to Madrona Island. Apparently, not a single person said they knew of a man named Trace working here, but there were several who knew this Tim, and because he seemed to match the description she gave, she's convinced Trace and Tim must be the same person. She also said it appears Tim is no longer on the island, but she can't quite bring herself to give up, and Madrona Island is the only clue she had."

"Seems like a pretty slim clue."

"It is," I agreed. "And if it wasn't for the fact that Harley is here to help us I'd say it was an impossible task." I looked at the cat. "So, how about it, big guy?

Do you have a starting point? Even a teeny, tiny, baby clue would be better than nothing."

Harley got off the table and trotted across the cabin, stopping in front of the coffee table I'd placed between the sofa and the fireplace. He stood patiently waiting, so I got up and joined him. The table was completely clear except for a peppermint-scented candle and the book of matches I used to light it. I doubted the candle was the clue, so I picked up the matchbook. Danny had left it the last time he was here. He didn't smoke cigarettes, but for some inexplicable reason he'd recently taken up smoking a pipe.

"Is this the clue?" I asked.

"Meow."

The matchbook was from a bar near the marina at Friday Harbor. I glanced at Cody. "We talked about a shopping trip. Should we try to get off work early and head over on the midday ferry?"

"I can make that work," Cody confirmed.

"I'll talk to Tara, but it should be fine. We'll have three hours on the island before we have to catch the last ferry back to Madrona. I say we start with the bar, then see where that takes us. If we have time we can do some shopping over there. If not, we'll do what we can when we get back."

"Sounds like a plan. I have an appointment with Jack Forrester this morning. I'm hoping I can work out some sort of a deal with him that will allow Burt to return to his home."

"So he lives on the island?"

"He lives in Seattle, but he's a real estate developer as well as a hard money lender and is on the island today to meet with a group of planners about a project he hopes to break ground on in the spring."

"Is he the guy who wants to build those tract houses up on the bluff?" I asked.

"One and the same."

"Siobhan told me the town council has some issues with the homes he's developing and has instructed the building department to wait before issuing the permits until they're resolved."

"Mr. Forrester did mention that part of the reason he's on the island is to work out the kinks in his plan. I don't suppose you know what the problems are exactly?"

"I don't have all the details, but it had to do with land coverage. If you want the details you should talk to Maggie. Even though she gave up her seat on the town council at the last election, she should know what's what. And Siobhan will know as well."

"I'll call them both. It's a good idea to go into any negotiation prepared with as much information as you can reasonably amass ahead of time."

******

The snow had started up again by the time I made it into the bookstore. Willow was dressed in one of the outfits Siobhan had given her and looked reasonably happy. I knew it gave her a certain piece of mind to have Harley and me helping her. I just hoped we didn't let her down.

I got the cats I'd brought settled in the cat lounge, then joined Tara and Willow in the bookstore.

"You didn't bring Harley?" Willow asked.

"I don't like to bring the cats who are here to help to the bookstore; they tend to attract the attention of people who want to adopt them."

"Do any of those cats ever need adopting?" Willow wondered.

"They all seem to know exactly where they're supposed to end up. When our missions are done I make sure they get there. Has it been busy this morning?"

"Not too bad with all the snow, but I expect things will pick up once the first ferry gets here," Tara answered. "Willow is helping me clean and restock the shelves; maybe you can make sure the coffee bar is ready for the first rush of the morning."

"Will do," I answered. "Cody and I are going over to San Juan Island on the midday ferry, so I'm going to ask Cassie to stop by later, pick up the cats, and take them back to the sanctuary. I think she was coming in this afternoon anyway to talk to you about helping out while she's on Christmas break."

"We could use the help," Tara answered. "Are you and Cody following up on a lead?"

I set the stack of cups I was unloading onto the counter. "Maybe. Harley led me to a matchbook Danny left at my cabin. I assume the bar the matchbook came from will lead to a clue, but Harley and I have just started working together, so I'm not sure I'm reading his actions as clearly as I should. It's just a short ferry ride over, so I may as well check things out. We'll be returning on the last ferry of the day and plan to do some Christmas shopping when we get back, but if Harley's hint leads to anything I'll be sure to call to let you both know." I looked at Willow. "Were you able to get a drawing of Trace?"

Willow nodded and handed me a piece of paper. "Tara really is a good artist. She knew just what to ask me. The drawing is pretty close."

I looked at the drawing and saw a man with shaggy brown hair, a thin face, and a short beard. "Tall or short?"

"Tall. At least six feet. He's thin, with blue eyes."

"Okay. This will help."

"I hope your lead pans out. I'd really like to have this resolved soon. I can't seem to relax with things being so uncertain, and I'm sure the stress isn't good for the baby."

"Have you been to a doctor?" Tara asked.

"No. I can't afford that."

"I thought you said the baby is a he?" I replied.

"I've been calling him that, but I don't know for certain."

"My boyfriend is a doctor. I'll ask Parker if he can slip you in for a checkup under the radar so you won't be billed," Tara offered.

"Are you sure he won't mind?" Willow asked.

"He won't mind," Tara assured her. "I'll call him now. Maybe he can see you today. It's a good idea to make sure everything is progressing as it should. You probably should be on prenatal vitamins as well."

Tara headed to the office to make the call and Willow returned to the shelves she was stocking. I felt so bad for the girl and really hoped we could help her find her happily ever after. I had to admit to feeling somewhat conflicted. Even if we did find Trace and he signed off on the adoption that would help the baby, it might not help Willow in the long run. Maybe while she was with us I could figure out a way to not only help the baby find his way into the family he was meant to be raised in, but I could also help Willow find a new start on life.

"Okay, you're all set," Tara said as she returned. "I'll take you over to see Parker on his lunch break."

"I hate to make him miss lunch," Willow said.

"He doesn't mind, and I'll bring him a sandwich. We should be back in plenty of time for Cait to make the midday ferry."

"Speaking of ferries, here comes the first one of the day," I announced. "Everyone man your battle stations," I joked.

******

Once the ferry crowd had cleared out and Tara and Willow had left for her doctor's appointment I took a minute to check in with Cody. He'd met with Mr. Forrester, who was willing to work out a deal with Burt in exchange for Cody paving the way for him to obtain the building permits he was after. The problem had to do with the number of homes he wanted to build on the land he'd purchased. Based on the current ordinance, only 60 percent of the surface area of any plot could be covered with permanent structures outside of the area designated for commercial enterprises. The town council had adopted this ordinance to maintain the rural feel of the island. Mr. Forrester wanted to maximize the land he'd bought for development by building a greater number of homes. His plan called for smaller yards and homes built much closer together than was currently allowed. To continue with his development, he'd require a variance, something the town council hadn't been inclined to grant.

When Cody first met with Mr. Forrester about Burt's home he hadn't seemed to be willing to even discuss the return of a house he'd ended up with for pennies on the dollar; when Cody let it slip that he was engaged to the sister of the mayor, suddenly he was all about mutual back scratching. Cody still had no idea how he could resolve the situation, but it was at least worth looking in to.

As for Willow and her situation, Cody hadn't come up with any new leads, but he was still game to take the midday ferry to San Juan Island, so he arranged to meet me at the bookstore at two-thirty. I restocked the coffee bar once again and was about to go down the hallway to the storage room when Cassie walked in with Alex.

"Look who I found loitering out front," Cassie teased.

"Alex," I cried as I hurried across the store for a hug. "I've missed you. How have you been?"

"I've been good. Great, actually."

I took a step back. "That's awesome. I'm so happy you're here for the holiday. We have to plan to get together for lunch or dinner. I'd suggest today, but I'm going over to San Juan Island on the midday ferry."

"Then another day for sure." Alex looked at his watch. "I should get going anyway. I hadn't planned to stop by today, but I saw Cassie out front and had to take a minute to say hi. I just arrived on the island and there's no food in my house, so I need to get to the market. Call me tomorrow and we'll figure out a time to get together."

"I will." I hugged Alex again, before he turned and headed to the door.

"Is Tara here?" Cassie asked after Alex left. "I wanted to talk to you both about a job."

"She took Willow for a doctor's appointment, but they should be back soon. If you aren't busy I could use some help restocking the coffee supplies."

"I assume I'm on the clock?"

I shrugged. "Sure, why not?"

******

Tara and Willow returned a few minutes before Cody arrived to catch the ferry. I didn't have a lot of time to ask questions, but I did find out Willow's baby was indeed a boy, as she suspected and I already knew, and he was in perfect health, which was a relief to us all. Parker had given Willow prenatal vitamins and another appointment in a month. I wasn't sure what Willow's long-term plans would be, but I'd been toying with the idea of talking to Tara about keeping her on past the holiday, at least until the baby was born. Broke and homeless was no way to be when you had a baby to consider.

"I think the bar is a block over," I said to Cody as we landed on San Juan Island. "Maybe we can grab something hot to drink while we're there. It's freezing today."

"A hot toddy does sound good. I hoped it would be warm enough to walk around and enjoy the Christmas decorations, but I have a feeling we're going to want to wait inside for the next ferry back to Madrona. I should have worn my heavier jacket."

"I have one in my car back at the bookstore. If we decide to go into town we can grab yours as well." I stopped walking and pointed down the street. "There."

We began walking again.

"Have you planned ahead for when we get there?" Cody asked.

"Not really," I admitted. "I guess we just strike up a conversation, then ask about Tim or Trace or whatever name he's using. Willow gave me a drawing Tara made of him, and I'm hoping someone will recognize him."

The bar was, thankfully, warm. It was nicely decorated, with garlands hanging from the bar and a tree in the corner. Cody and I sat down at the bar and ordered Irish coffees. Soft jazz played in the background, providing a cozy feeling to the already welcoming atmosphere.

"Can I get you folks anything else?" the bartender asked after setting our beverages in front of us.

"Actually, I was hoping you could help me find a friend I'm trying to track down," I answered. "His name is Trace and he worked on Madrona Island this summer. I understand he might have been using the name Tim while he was here." I slipped the man the drawing.

"We get a lot of folks coming in and out during the summer, but he does look familiar. Can you tell me anything else that might help him stand out in my mind?"

"I've been told he worked for a fishing operation based in Alaska for a while, though that lead didn't pan out."

"Alaska? Any chance he worked for a cargo hauler?"

"I don't know. He might have. Unfortunately, we don't know much."

"I can't be sure, but I remember talk of a kid named Tim who got himself mixed up in some dirty business involving a company that transported people and smaller yet more valuable cargo between the islands and Alaska. If the guy you're looking for is the one I'm thinking of you should talk to Blackburn. He runs a cargo transport operation out of the local marina. Deals in high-dollar transports for customers willing to pay cash."

"So, illegal property?"

"I didn't say that, and you might not want to either. Still, if your friend was hauling cargo Blackburn would know about it."

"Where can I find him?"

"Lives in a cabin near the marina. Go down to the end of this street, turn left when you get to the marina, and follow the road to the end. You can tell him I sent you, but whatever you do, don't ask him about his own operation. Blackburn doesn't take kindly to people nosing around in his business."

"Understood."

Cody slipped the bartender forty dollars and we were heading to the door when a man stumbled into the bar. He was totally hammered and certainly didn't need another drink. I was about to step around him when he changed direction and bumped into me, almost knocking me to the floor. Cody grabbed my arm and steadied me. I was about to make a remark about his inebriated state when I realized he was the man Tara had hired to play Santa for Coffee Cat Books beginning the next day.

"You're Bruce Littleton."

"Yeah. What's it to you?"

Cody grabbed my arm and led me out the door before I could respond.

"What's with the manhandling?" I complained as he pulled me out into the cold.

"The guy was drunk and not thinking straight. I could tell by his body language that he was looking for a fight. I've seen it before. There are some guys who consider slugging it out with a total stranger to be some sort of therapeutic release. I'm sure I could have taken him if I'd been forced to engage, but I'm just as happy to avoid the confrontation altogether."

"I guess you're right. I need to call Tara, though. There's no way that drunk is going to be our Santa."

Tara confirmed that she'd verbally offered Bruce the job when he'd applied a few days earlier, but they hadn't gotten around to filling out any paperwork. After I told her about the confrontation we agreed she'd call to tell him we were going in a different direction and his services wouldn't be required after all. Of course, that left us short a Santa, but I reminded her that Alex, who had been the best one we'd ever had, was in town. Perhaps he wouldn't mind helping us out for old time's sake. Tara agreed to ask him.

Once that was settled, Cody and I headed to the marina. There were flurries in the air that were pretty, but I couldn't help but long for the warmth of a crackling fire and a warm throw to snuggle under. Maybe Cody and I would just go back to my place when we got back to Madrona. The idea of cuddling under a blanket while we shared our dreams for the future was sounding better and better with every minute that passed.

Unlike most of the other buildings in town, Blackburn's cabin lacked even the most basic of holiday decorations. It was getting dark and the blinds were drawn, but I saw a light shining through the crack between them, so we climbed the shabby stairs and knocked.

"Yeah?" a rough-looking man with yellowed teeth and a large scar on his cheek answered.

"My name is Caitlin Hart and this is Cody West. We're looking for a friend and was told you might have seen him." He just stared at me, so I continued. "I call him Trace, but I understand he could be using the name Tim. He might have worked for a cargo transport company that operated out of the marina over the summer, although we aren't certain."

"Skinny kid with a mop of dark hair?"

"Yeah, that sounds like him. Do you happen to know where he might be now?"

"I'm guessing dead."

My breath caught in my throat. "Dead?"

"Kid was too big for his britches. It's my understanding one of my competitors hired him on for a few long hauls. From what I heard, the kid was full of bad ideas and decided to do some transporting on the side. Most folks who hire a person to work on their behalf don't take kindly to their employees cutting them out of whatever jobs might come their way."

"Do you know what Tim was transporting?"

Blackburn shrugged. "Probably drugs or stolen goods. I don't have all the details; I just heard some of my men talking about the fact that some dumb kid had come to the area thinking he was smarter than the man he worked for, but it turned out he was wrong."

"Do you know the name of the man Tim might have worked for?"

"Goes by Trout, but I wouldn't be asking him about your friend if I were you. Lots of ways to end up dead. Stealing from your boss is one of them; asking the wrong person the wrong question is another."

Chapter 6

"What do you make of that?" Cody asked as we rode the ferry back to Madrona Island.

"I don't know, but I think I need to talk to Aiden and Danny. They both own boats and know all the local players. I suppose I should have brought them in on this from the beginning. They might even have met Tim at some point over the summer."

"Yeah, that's a good idea. I know we're trying to keep things quiet, but I have a feeling quiet isn't going to help us find the guy."

"I'm not sure I even want to. I'm afraid our search for the father of Willow's baby won't have a happy ending if Trace is dead. I hate to even suggest such a thing to Willow until we know for sure one way or another."

"So don't. At least not until we know more. We don't even know with one hundred percent certainty that Trace and Tim are the same person."

I looked out the window and watched as the falling snow hit the water. The heat from the overhead vent combined with the loud, steady hum of the ferry engine left me feeling lethargic, but my mind was in such turmoil I knew I'd never be able to relax enough to actually rest.

Cody put his arm around my shoulders and pulled me close. "Do you still want to go shopping?"

I turned to look at the man I loved. "Honestly, no. I think I'd rather head back to the cabin, build a fire, put on some music, and make that list we never got around to last night. Danny and Aiden should both be at Maggie's; maybe we can pick their brains as well."

"Do we need to stop by the bookstore to pick up the cats?" Cody asked.

"Cassie's bringing them home. She's off on break for the next two weeks and is going to work at the bookstore, so she offered to help out with the cats anytime I needed her."

"That will help. It's hard to know how things are going to work out, but it seems helping Willow has the potential to become pretty complicated."

"It really does seem that way. I was thinking…" My thought was interrupted by the ringing of my phone. I looked at the caller ID before I answered. "Hey, Tara, what's up?"

"Parker and I are going to grab a bite to eat. I figured the last ferry would be docking in the next ten minutes. Do you want to join us?"

I considered taking Tara up on her offer, then decided I was too cold and tired to go out for dinner. "I think we'll pass tonight. I didn't get a lot of sleep last night and am pretty beat. Another time, though.

"How'd it go on San Juan? Did your lead pan out?"

"Maybe. Cody and I found out that someone named Tim worked for a local cargo hauler named Trout. We don't know that Tim and Trace are the same guy, but in the event they are, Cody and I plan to follow up with him. We've been led to understand he's the sort who doesn't like people poking around in his business, so we thought we'd have a chat with Aiden and Danny when we get back to the cabin. They know all the people who operate in this area."

"As long as you're talking to them, show them the drawing and ask them if they recognize him. If he worked on the water at all, chances are one of them ran into him at some point. Also, Willow remembered something Trace told her back in Seattle that may help. He told her that he chose to work on Madrona for the summer because his grandfather had told him so many amazing stories about the island. After she thought about it she said he made it sound like the grandfather had lived here at some point, although he'd since passed on."

"If he lived on the island that could be helpful, but without a name I don't know how good a lead it is."

"I know it's a long shot, but Trace said his grandfather was a carpenter who was known for his unique furniture designs. There aren't a lot of furniture designers in the islands, so it might be possible to find the name of a carpenter who lived here around the time Trace was a kid."

"It wouldn't hurt to ask around. Maggie might have an idea who we're looking for. If we could identify the grandfather that might help us figure out the legal first and last name of the man who fathered

Willow's baby. If we can do that we might have success with a Google search."

"That's what I thought. Will you be in tomorrow?"

"I'm planning on it. I'll call you if something comes up, but for now I'll see you in the morning." I hung up and turned to Cody. "Tara has a lead regarding Trace's grandfather that may pan out."

"We may as well follow all the clues we come up with to their natural conclusion. The ferry's about to dock. Let's head down to the car."

******

We picked up a pizza with the works and drove to my cabin. I let Max out for a quick run while Cody built a fire, plugged in the Christmas tree, lit some candles, and put on some music. By the time we returned the pizza had been warmed and the wine was open. We had the perfect setup for an evening of romance. Too bad we had work to do.

"While Max and I were out, I noticed everyone's car is in the drive, which means everyone's staying in tonight. I know we didn't want to bring too many people in on what we're up to, but we're planning to talk to Danny and Aiden and Cassie and Siobhan already know at least part of what we're doing, so I think we should just go ahead and bring everyone up to speed. Finn really should be in the loop, especially if it turns out this Trout guy is involved, and Maggie always has her finger on the pulse of all the gossip on the island."

"Fine," Cody said. "We don't need to mention the fact that Willow's baby will grow up to play an important role in the future, but I don't see the harm in letting the others in on the fact that we're trying to find the baby's father so she can proceed with the adoption."

"Okay, let's eat and then go over to Maggie's. Siobhan is a wiz at keeping us all organized; maybe if we put our heads together we can figure out where the baby daddy is."

When Cody and I arrived at Maggie's everyone was gathered in the living room watching a Christmas movie. The movie, which I'd seen before, had only about fifteen minutes remaining, so I sat on the floor near Danny's feet while Cody pulled a barstool up behind the sofa. As soon as the credits began to roll, I asked them if they'd be willing to help us with something we were working on. Before I could say *Ghost of Christmas Future*, Siobhan was on her way upstairs, dragging Finn and Danny behind her, to grab a whiteboard and the other things we'd need.

"I was hoping you'd decide to bring us in on whatever's going on with Willow," Siobhan said as she took her place in front of the whiteboard.

"It's sort of a delicate situation, so I needed to check out a few things first, but I think you can all be helpful," I answered. "Willow came to the island to find the father of her baby. We don't have a lot to go on because she didn't know him well, but finding him is important because he has to sign off on the adoption Willow has arranged."

"She isn't going to keep him?" Siobhan's face fell.

"She's told me she wants the baby to have the best opportunities in life, and she knows she isn't going be able to provide them herself."

"That may be true, but it's still sad," Siobhan said. "I don't want to turn this into a debate on the pros and cons of adoption, though. I take it you don't have any real leads or you wouldn't be here."

"You're mostly correct. Here's what we know." I started off by briefly sharing the things Willow had followed up on when she first arrived on the island. I discussed her failed trip to Seward, as well as her conviction that Trace might still be in the area, and segued to our trip to the bar on San Juan Island. Then I asked Aiden and Danny if either of them had run into anyone named either Trace or Tim over the summer.

"I do know of a guy named Tim who worked here over the summer," Danny said. "He seemed to hop around. I know he was on a fishing boat for a while, and I seem to remember him hooking up with a whale-watch tour after that. Do you have a photo?"

I passed the drawing to him. "Tara drew this from Willow's description."

Danny looked at the paper. "This isn't him. The guy I'm thinking of had a fuller face and thicker eyebrows. Do you know if the man Willow's looking for spoke with an accent?"

"She didn't mention one."

"Tim definitely has an accent. Southern, I think. It isn't very heavy, but it comes through when he's had a few too many."

"Have you seen this Tim recently?"

Danny shook his head. "Not since the season wrapped up and I leased out my boat."

"Do you remember where he worked?"

"Like I said, he hopped around. He did a few weeks with Cap Collins and then headed north. I think I heard he got on with a crabbing boat out of Homer, Alaska, but I don't know that for certain. At some point I heard he was subbing for A Whale of a Tour out of Harthaven. I'm not sure that amounted to much, though."

It was beginning to sound as if Tim and Trace weren't the same person after all. Given the link to Trout, I hoped that was true.

"Cody and I spoke to a man named Blackburn, who told us that Tim hooked up with a cargo hauler named Trout. According to Blackburn, Tim tried to smuggle his own cargo on the side. Blackburn heard Trout found out and might have killed him."

"Yep, that fits," Danny said. "Trout wouldn't take kindly to someone trying to cheat him out of what he considered to be his." Danny looked at Finn, who was frowning. "Of course, if Tim cheated Trout and Trout killed him in retaliation, you'll never find the body or any proof. Trout's a tough one. He's been around for a lot of years and knows how to get someone gone. Folks around the islands know that if you sign on with Trout you best play it on the up and up."

"Okay, wait," Siobhan said, dry-erase marker in hand. "Are we saying the father of Willow's baby is dead?"

"If the man we're looking for and the one who cheated Trout are the same person, yeah, it's a possibility," I answered and then paused. "How do we prove any of this? How do we figure out if Trace and Tim are the same person? And if they are, how do we prove Tim cheated Trout and ended up dead because of it? All we have is one person who heard a rumor from his men."

"I can find out if someone named Tim worked for Trout," Danny offered. "I can even find out if he cheated Trout out of money that should have been his."

"Sounds dangerous," Mom said.

"Don't worry. I know the rules. I'll ask around, but I won't push."

"We need a photo of Trace," Aiden joined in.

"We don't even know his last name, but we do have a lead on that. Willow said Trace told her that his grandfather used to live on the island. He was a carpenter who was famous for the unique furniture he designed."

"Buck Barrington," Maggie said.

"You knew him?"

"Sure. Everyone knew Buck. He had a real talent. See that table in the entry?" Maggie pointed toward the front door. "Buck made it for me over twenty years ago."

"So, if Buck Barrington was Trace's grandfather on his father's side, we might have a last name. If Trace really is the first name of the man who sired Willow's baby, we should be able to dig up a photograph of him."

"The name Buck Barrington sounds familiar, but I can't quite place it," Finn said.

"He died quite a while ago," Maggie offered. "He was shot during a robbery."

"I do remember something about that. It was before my time, but there'll be a file. I'll take a look. And I'll run the name Trace Barrington through the sheriff's database to see what I can find."

"Buck's wife still lives on the island," Maggie volunteered. "Actually, the woman I'm thinking of was his second wife. His first wife passed on years ago. Still, if we're lucky she'll have Buck's old photo albums. Maybe we can find a photo of Trace, if he's really Buck's grandson. I'll call her tomorrow to see if she's willing to meet with you."

"Thanks, Maggie. That would be great."

Maybe we'd find a way to track down the father of Willow's baby after all.

******

"What a day," I said later that evening as we relaxed by the fire with a glass of wine.

"It does feel like life has taken on a complicated twist," Cody agreed. "Hopefully, Mrs. Barrington will know where Trace is or can send us in his direction even if she doesn't."

"Yeah, hopefully." I yawned. "I never did ask if you were able to come up with any additional information that might help us get Burt back into his house."

"I spoke to each of the town council members. The opinion is pretty much split. On one side of the debate you have council members who want to find a way to provide affordable housing on the island. On the other are those who want to see the integrity of the rural feel of the island protected. It's an ongoing debate. We saw the same thing played out a few years ago with the condo project that ended up being scraped."

"It's a complex issue," I agreed.

"My sense is that unless a new plan, a new perspective, or new information comes forth, the issue will remain stalemated. Because it takes a three-quarter vote to approve a variance or change a previously set ordinance, the reality is that having more than one no vote shuts everything down."

I frowned. "While I want to help Burt, I'm not sure allowing some big housing tract to be developed is the right way to go, even if we could convince enough council members to go along with the idea."

Cody let out a slow breath. "It's a complicated subject. And I agree, it would be a shame if Madrona Island turned into just another urban area. Having said that, there really is a need for affordable housing here. Once the ferry began to dock here, making the trip easy for visitors from Seattle, the change from single-family residences to vacation homes and rentals has been dramatic. Most of the people who grew up here and want to live here year-round can't afford to buy a home and are moving to areas where home ownership is affordable."

I took a sip of my wine. Cody had a point, but the folks who didn't want to see the small-town feel of our island become more of a big city like Honolulu had a point as well. "What are you thinking?"

Cody set down his glass, turned, and looked at me. "If you look at the land Forrester owns in isolation, and the number of units he wants to build, it just doesn't work. Under the current land coverage rules, once streets, sidewalks, and other infrastructure is accounted for, you have allowable coverage left to build forty-eight homes, each with a footprint of about a thousand square feet. He told me that unless he can build seventy-two units he won't be able to offer the discount he intends. If he can't make a certain amount of profit he'll most likely be forced to move on to another project."

"Seventy-two homes? He really does plan to pack them in, doesn't he?"

Cody nodded. "The yards will be small and the houses will be built using what's known as a zero-clearance property line. What that means is that one wall of each house will serve as the property line for its neighbor. It's just one step up from condos."

"Sounds awful."

"To you and me maybe, but I'm betting to a lot of young families who figured they'd never be able to buy a home on the island, even one in a tightly built community would be a welcome opportunity."

I wasn't a fan of tract homes in general, but I supposed Cody had a point. Housing really was an issue on the island. "Are you going to try to get the council members who oppose the project on board? I don't think it'll be that easy to do. Once you make a variance for one project you set a precedent, and I don't think anyone wants to see a trend like zero property line housing to get a foothold here."

"I completely agree," Cody said. "Which is why I came up with a compromise of sorts."

"A compromise?"

Cody sat back, seeming to gather his thoughts before he began. "The current ordinance allows only sixty percent of any parcel of land to be developed. That sixty percent must include all hard cover, including homes, streets, sidewalks, even patios. Because the ordinance originated from a desire to protect the rural feel of the island, the rules were very tightly written. What isn't spelled out, however, is the equality by which the coverage is distributed."

"Huh?"

"Let's say you have a parcel that measures a hundred square feet. Any lot would be larger than that, of course, but a hundred square feet is easy to use for the purposes of demonstration."

"Yeah, okay. Go on."

"The current ordinance allows for coverage of sixty percent or sixty square feet. Theoretically, you can have one building with a footprint of sixty square feet, or you can have three smaller buildings with a footprint of twenty square feet each or some other distribution. I suppose you could even have sixty really small buildings with a footprint of one square foot. The only rule is that the total land coverage can't be more than sixty percent of the total area of the plot to land."

"Okay, that makes sense."

"I've been thinking about the situation and it seems to me that the way to meet both Forrester's needs and the land coverage limits without a variance would be to throw additional land in to the mix."

"Come again?"

"For simplicity's sake, based on our previous hundred-square-foot plot of land, if you want to cover seventy-two feet instead of sixty you just need to make the original plot larger."

"So, you're saying Forrester should buy additional land?"

"No. That would ruin his profit margin, so it won't work. But what if we could get the person who owns the land adjacent to the land Forrester plans to build on to donate the land for a park? Then all we have to do is convince the council to consider the land Forrester wants to develop and the undeveloped land reserved for a park as a single unit in terms of land coverage."

Okay. It would be one large tract of land with all the structures on just half of it. "Who owns the land that would have to be donated?"

"Olivia Stanwell."

Olivia Stanwell was a descendent of one of the founding fathers and owned quite a bit of land on the island. She was opinionated and somewhat self-serving and, in my opinion, unlikely to donate any of her land to help an out-of-area developer, and I told Cody as much. Still, the idea addressed a multitude of issues. If Olivia could be convinced to donate the land Forrester could build his zero clearance homes, which would attract young couples just starting out. If the council looked at both the land owned by Forrester and the land donated by Olivia as a single unit he wouldn't need a variance to build his development, thus eliminating the problem of setting a precedent. Plus, the island would end up with a nice park.

"So, what's your plan?" I asked.

"I'm meeting with Olivia tomorrow and I'll see where our conversation takes us."

"Have you broached the subject at all with her yet?"

He shook his head. "I just said I was doing an article for the newspaper and had some questions for her, and she agreed to see me. I figure once I get her in the room I can figure out a way to ask her about donating the land. I know it'll be a hard sell, but it's the only idea I have."

"It's a good one. I hope she'll consider it. While cookie-cutter homes don't thrill me, you make a good point about the housing crisis in the area. I think it can help everyone in the long run."

"I hope so." Cody put his arm around my shoulder and pulled me close. "Do you still want to watch that movie?"

"I think I'd rather head upstairs. It's late and I'm exhausted."

"Too exhausted?"

I smiled. "Well, maybe not *that* exhausted."

Chapter 7

Saturday, December 16

By the time I arrived at Coffee Cat Books the next morning Tara and Willow were already working behind the counter of the coffee bar and Cassie and Alex were busy decorating the area set aside for Santa's chair. I glanced at the clock, which confirmed I wasn't late, so everyone else must have been early. It was a busy time of year, so I guess I understood why the others felt the need to get an early start, but when you wake up wrapped in the arms of the man you love and plan to marry, getting up early is the last thing you want to do.

"Oh good, you're here," Tara greeted me. "Did you bring the cats?"

"I have four in the car. I'll bring them in and get them settled."

"Do you have any kittens today? Betty Harrington was in with her daughter, Bethany, and they want to adopt a kitten. Orange-striped, if you have one, if not gray and white will do. I texted to let you know they'd popped in, but you were probably already on the road by then."

I pulled out my phone and glanced at the unread text. "Yeah, I didn't see it. I didn't bring kittens today, but I do have them. Did they seem intent on looking at them today?"

Tara nodded. "Bethany has been waiting for her tenth birthday. Her mom made her a deal that she could get a kitten when she turned ten if she kept her grades up, which she has."

"And today is her birthday?"

Tara nodded once again.

"Okay, I'll call them. It might be easier to have them meet me at the cat sanctuary. I've known Betty for years, so the normal screening won't be necessary. If they can meet me I'll get the cats I brought settled, run back to the sanctuary to help them with a kitten, and be back in plenty of time to meet the first ferry."

"That sounds good. Did the lead you were working on for Willow work out?"

"Maybe. I'll fill everyone in after I get back."

Normally, I would have asked a prospective cat parent to meet me at the cat sanctuary after work, but it seemed Bethany had been wanting a kitten for a long time and I was sure it would make her birthday all that much special not to have to wait any longer. My mom was at Maggie's today, keeping an eye on Aiden, but she didn't have a lot of patience with the cats, and I wanted to make sure Bethany was matched with the perfect kitten.

When I got to the sanctuary Betty and Bethany were already there. Bethany took her time, holding all the kittens, and eventually settled on a black and white tuxedo who purred so loudly when she picked him up that it startled us all. I helped Betty fill out the necessary paperwork, then headed back to my car only to find Harley sitting on the hood.

"How did you get out here?"

"Meow."

I picked up the furry cat. "I need to get back to work. Can whatever it is you want to show me wait?"

"Meow."

"I didn't think so." I set the cat on the ground. "Okay, what is it you want me to see?"

Harley sat patiently next to the passenger side door. It seemed obvious he wanted to go with me. Cody had taken Max with him to the newspaper, so I had to figure my Ebenezer lookalike wasn't happy about being left at home alone.

"Okay," I said as I opened the door and waited for the cat to jump in. "You can come with me, but you need to hang out in the office or behind the coffee bar where you won't attract too much attention."

Harley looked totally content as he settled into the passenger seat, as I started the engine, pulled away from the driveway, and headed back to town.

"You brought Harley." Willow grinned the minute he walked through the front door.

"He rather insisted. I don't want him in the cat lounge, where I'll have to continually explain why he, unlike the other cats, isn't available for adoption. I'm going to see if he'll hang out in the office."

"I think he might have other ideas." Alex laughed as Harley jumped into the Santa chair and sat regally looking around the room.

"Maybe if we bring in one of the cat beds he'll be content in a corner of the shop where he'll be less likely to get trampled," Cassie suggested.

"Good idea. Or maybe we can have him sit next to Santa. He can be Santa Cat, Mr. Claus's new mascot."

Willow came around from the far side of the bar and picked up the cat. "My back is beginning to hurt, so Tara suggested I lay down on the sofa in the office until the ferry gets here. I'll bring him with me while you all decide the rest."

"She looks so tired," Alex said as he watched Willow walk down the hall with the cat.

"She's had a rough time, but I think things will improve now that she's staying with Tara," I answered.

"Did the lead about Trace's grandfather pan out?" Tara asked.

"Maybe. Maggie knows the widow of the man we believe to have been Trace's grandfather. I have an appointment to see her at one. I figured that's a slowish time of day, so hopefully you won't miss me too much if I have to be gone for an hour. If her husband was the man Trace told Willow about, maybe there's something that will help us narrow in on where he was when he came to the island. If nothing else, I'm hoping we can find a photo. I'll feel better if I know for certain Trace and Tim weren't the same person as we first thought."

******

Cora Barrington lived in a pretty yellow house with white shutters just a block from the ocean. When she answered the door I was surprised to find she was much younger than I would have thought. She was Buck's second wife, though, so I supposed she didn't have to be old enough to be Trace's grandmother.

"Hi. I'm Cait Hart. My aunt called to ask if you had a few minutes to speak with me."

"Yes. Come on in."

The house was lovely inside too. The walls were pale yellow with white crown molding and the floors were all hardwood that looked as if they had been recently waxed. Despite the fact that there was snow on the ground outside, there were bouquets of fresh flowers on several tables, and the white furniture was so clean it looked as if it had never been used.

"How can I help you?" Cora asked, motioning toward the sofa.

I sat carefully on the edge, not wanting to get cat hair, which I was sure was on my clothing, on the lovely fabric. "I guess my aunt told you that I'm helping a friend locate the father of her baby. Willow only knew him briefly and the only name she has is Trace. They met in Seattle, and it was only after he'd left that she realized she was pregnant. She plans to put the baby up for adoption but would like to notify the father first. The only thing she has to go on, other than that first name, is that he told her he was heading to Madrona Island to work on a fishing boat and that the reason he wanted to come here was because his grandfather, who was a carpenter, had told him wonderful stories about it. Trace told Willow that his grandfather built furniture and my aunt said Buck had been in the business."

"So you think the young man you're looking for could be Buck's grandson?"

"That's what we're hoping."

"Buck had a son, Chris, but I never met him. When Buck's first wife died and he began dating me, Chris was upset that his father could replace his mother so quickly, and the two argued. Eventually, they worked out something of a peace, and Buck went to Chicago every year to visit his son and grandson, but they never came here."

"Do you have any photos that belonged to Buck?"

"There are some things in the attic. Buck has been gone for eight years so I wouldn't have any recent photos, but I suppose even an old photo might tell you if the man you're looking for was Buck's grandson. His name is Bryce, however, not Trace."

"We suspect Trace may have been a nickname. Would you mind if I looked at any photos Buck left?"

"Not at all. I'll show you what I have."

The attic was dusty and musty. It didn't look like anyone had been up there in a long time. Cora led me back to a corner and showed me a stack of boxes. She told me that I was free to look through them, but the dust bothered her sinuses, so she'd wait for me downstairs.

As I hoped, the boxes contained photos and other mementos of Buck's life with his first wife. There were quite a few photos of a dark-haired woman I assumed was her, standing with a dark-haired boy at various stages of his life. If I was going to prove Bryce or Trace were the same person I'd have to find something more recent, so I moved on to the next box, hoping it contained them. I was halfway through the second box when Tara called.

"Hey, what's up?"

"Your cat is going bonkers."

"Which cat?" I asked.

"Your witchy cat. Harley. He was sleeping with Willow on the sofa and then Finn came in, looking for you. When I told him you weren't here he said he'd call you later. Before he left he said he'd found out that someone named Bryce Barrington had recently been in jail in Homer, Alaska. He was arrested last Tuesday for engaging in a bar fight and released yesterday."

"Did Finn have a photo of Bryce?"

"I didn't ask him, but he might have his mug shot."

"Okay. I'll head over to his office to see if he does. I'll be at the bookstore after that."

I explained to Cora that I had to go but still might want to come by to continue my search. She said she was fine with me taking the boxes I still needed to look through, and if I found Bryce I could pass the photos on to him. If I didn't, I agreed to bring them back to her. She didn't seem to be sentimentally attached to the photos, so I loaded up my car and headed to Finn's office. When I arrived he printed me a copy of the photo taken when Bryce was booked and I took it to the bookstore.

The moment Willow saw the photo she started to cry. The man had a cut lip and a black eye, but Bryce Barrington was the father of her baby. "I need to go to Homer," she insisted.

"You shouldn't go alone. There's no way to know if Bryce is still there, and even if he is, there's no way to predict his state of mind."

Harley jumped into Alex's lap and began pawing his face. It might have been because he was wearing the Santa beard, but I had a feeling it had more to do with him wanting Alex to go with Willow.

"It looks like Harley wants me to accompany our fair maiden in distress," Alex joked.

"Call me a maiden one more time and you'll be the one in distress," Willow shot back.

"Ouch." Alex set the cat on the floor. "I'm sorry. I shouldn't tease you, but I'm willing to take you north. I know a guy with a private charter service. If his jet is available we can leave today."

Willow frowned. "You would do that? You would charter a plane just to help me?"

Alex shrugged. "Sure. I don't have anything more pressing to do. The bookstore is closed on Sundays and Mondays, so if we leave after closing I won't even have to bail on my Santa duty."

Willow glanced at me.

I nodded. "I think it's a good idea to go with Alex. Tara and I can continue to look for clues here, just in case the trail goes cold. For all we know, Bryce was just passing through when he was arrested. It's possible he's heading back in this direction as we speak. It's best to have our bases covered."

Willow hesitated, then glanced once again at Alex. It looked as if she was having a hard time making up her mind whether to go with Alex, but eventually, she agreed. Alex took a break from his Santa duties to call his friend. If he was available they would leave either that night or the next morning.

Chapter 8

Later that evening, Cody and I sat at my dining table looking for additional clues in the boxes I'd borrowed from Cora. Alex's friend hadn't been available until the following morning, so they planned to get a good night's sleep, then head out at first light. As it turned out, Harley had a fit when Alex and Willow tried to leave without him, so Alex called his friend back to ask if he was okay with the cat going with them, then called a hotel to make sure they were fine with the cat as well. In the end, it was a party of three planning to head north.

The really interesting thing wasn't that Harley had insisted on going along; it was that Alex had suggested it would be easiest if Willow stayed at his place tonight and she'd agreed. I had to admit it surprised me because Willow had been so hesitant to go with him in the first place, though I'd noticed her watching him with Harley while he completed his Santa shift. It occurred to me that somewhere along the line she'd decided if Harley trusted Alex she could too.

The other piece of good news was that I'd shown Danny the photo of Bryce and he'd verified that Bryce/Trace and Tim, who we suspected may have met with an unpleasant end, weren't the same person. I felt bad I wasn't more concerned about what had happened to Tim, but I didn't know him and I already had my hands full with helping Willow and the holidays to plan for. Finn did say he'd look in to the rumors about Tim to see if he could verify what the local fishermen were saying.

"I'm a little surprised Buck's widow let you take these boxes," Cody said as we sorted and stacked the contents.

"She said Buck's son was angry when they started dating. She never even met him. I have a feeling she was just as glad to be rid of the reminder of the part of Buck's life that didn't include her. I'm sure it must have hurt each year when Buck went to Chicago to visit with his family and she wasn't invited."

"Yeah, I can see that." Cody stopped what he was doing and looked at me. "As interesting as sorting through all this is, I'm not sure why we're still looking for photos. We already know Bryce and Trace are the same person. Buck died before Trace left home, so I don't think we'll find any clues relating to that."

"It probably is a waste of time to continue to go through the boxes." I raised my hands over my head and stretched out the kink that was forming in my shoulder. "By the way, were you able to see Olivia today?"

"I was."

"And...?"

"And she's willing to consider donating the land for the park, but she wants something in return."

Figures. "So what did Olivia, who already has more than most, want in exchange for the land?"

"She wanted the park to be named after her grandfather, which shouldn't be a problem, and she wanted us to track down her daughter Rosemary and convince her to come home for Christmas."

"Track her down? She doesn't know where she is?"

Cody shook his head. "The two had a falling-out when she found out Rosemary was pregnant by a man she barely knew. Olivia wanted her to put the baby up for adoption, but Rosemary insisted on keeping the baby. She said she hasn't spoken to her daughter for ten years, but now that time has passed and she's gained some perspective, she realizes how silly the fight was. She wants the opportunity to reconcile with her daughter and meet her granddaughter. I reminded her that Christmas was less than two weeks away and finding her daughter might not be all that easy. She of course reminded me that you tracked down Balthazar Pottage's son, who had been missing for more than twenty years, in less time than that, and was confident you'd come through once again."

I narrowed my brow. "So in order to save Buck's house we have to find a way to convince the island council to approve Jack Forrester's project, the best way to get the council on board being to bundle in open area to serve as a public park, but in order to do that we need Olivia to donate some of her land, which she's willing to do if we can locate the daughter she's estranged from?"

"Exactly."

"How on earth are we supposed to do all that and help Willow and get ready for what's turning out to be a huge Christmas Eve party?"

"I don't know. But I think we have to try to do what we can. The more I think about it, providing both affordable housing and a nice public park is a good cause even if you consider it in isolation."

"It is a good plan. Did you ask Maggie or Siobhan if they thought it would work if you could get Olivia to donate the land?"

"I asked Siobhan about it and she thought she could help me sell the idea. Of course, we won't really know how the council will feel about it until we can secure a commitment from Olivia to donate the land, and she didn't seem to be willing to do that until we found her daughter."

"I'd like to help Olivia reconcile with her daughter whether the plan to help Buck get his house back falls into place or not. I'm just feeling a little overwhelmed."

"Me too. We need a break. How about we get bundled up and go to the candle ceremony as planned? We can grab some dinner and maybe even do some shopping after."

I smiled. "Sounds good. Just let me change into a heavier sweater and my warmer boots."

******

The candle ceremony had been a holiday tradition on Madrona Island since before I was born. It all began when my dad was just a boy and a huge storm ripped through the islands just before Christmas.

When the storm had dissipated it left the entire island without electricity on Christmas Eve. Those of us who make the island home are a tough bunch, so instead of wallowing in self-pity that Christmas was ruined, the entire population gathered together, lit candles, and sang carols by candlelight.

Things were back to normal by the following year, but the tradition of gathering together to light candles and sing carols continued. Initially, the ceremony was held on Christmas Eve, but most families had their own traditions on this most special of nights, so the ceremony was moved around a bit before finding a home in the middle of the month. It made sense that the candles would be lit midmonth; the annual tree lighting was at the beginning of the month and there were a lot of events held right before the holiday, so most folks could find time to attend in the middle.

This year Cody and I were going alone. It was the first time I'd gone without at least a few members of my family, but I found I was looking forward to an intimate evening. Because the other Hart siblings had plans and Maggie was going with Father Kilian, Mom had decided to stay home with Aiden and watch Christmas movies.

It really didn't work to plunge the entire island into darkness as they'd been that first time, so the ceremony was held in the park at the center of Harthaven and only the lights in the immediate area were turned off for the thirty-minute event. When the lights came back on a lot of us got together for dinner or went into town to look through the shop windows, so Cody and I were expecting to have to deal with crowded conditions. Not that we cared. It was fun to walk around the crowded streets hand in hand, pausing to look at the holiday displays. It was even fun to have to wait for a table once we reached Antonio's. The people who'd gathered outside to wait for their number to be called brought a positive energy to what could have been a tense and frustrating situation.

"Cait, Cody, how are you both?" Jennifer Conroy, owner of the Harthaven Inn, asked as we wandered toward the group she was a part of.

"We're good. Were you at the candle ceremony?" I asked conversationally.

"Yes. It was moving as always. I'm glad we don't have to deal with a storm at Christmas, but I can imagine it must have been magical when residents from all around the island gathered on that first Christmas Eve."

"It must have been something special."

"Are the two of you here alone?" Jennifer asked.

"Everyone else had plans tonight, so it's just Cody and me. It was just as well because we plan to do some shopping later, and the people who usually accompany me are the ones I still need to buy gifts for."

"I hear you. It's been such a busy season so far. I feel like my to-do list is so impossibly long I'll never get to everything, but I guess it's that way most years."

"True. I wanted to buy something special for Finn and Siobhan's baby and hoped to make it into Seattle, but it looks like that isn't going to happen."

"I wouldn't worry about it too much. The baby isn't even born yet. You have time to be the fun and thoughtful aunt. By the way, now that I've run into you, I wanted to suggest the inn for the out-of-town guests who may fly in for your wedding. If you're able to come up with a date early enough, I can reserve a block of rooms that I'll, of course, provide to your guests at a deep discount."

"The inn is lovely and I'm sure our guests would love to stay there, but we don't have a date yet. When we do I'll check back with you. How much lead time do you think you'll need?"

"It depends. If you're thinking of getting married in July or August I'd need to know in the next few weeks; we fill up fast for the summer. If you decide on the off-season a few months' notice should be fine. Except for the two weeks around Christmas, Valentine's Day, and to a certain extent Thanksgiving weekend, I usually always have vacancies between October and May. In fact, I mostly only have weekend visitors except for a few people, like the man Finn was looking for, who rent a room for an entire month."

I raised a brow. "Trace Barrington is staying at the inn?"

"He said his name was Bryce, but Barrington is correct. Finn showed me a photo and I confirmed he's staying with me, although I haven't seen him in a week."

"How long has he been with you?" I asked.

"Since the beginning of December. He's planning to head out after the first of the year, but he had some business in town, so he's booked through the month. He'd just come off a fishing gig and had a pocketful of money. He seemed like a nice kid, so I agreed to the monthly rate despite the Christmas holiday. I hope he's not in any sort of trouble."

"No. A friend of ours needed to find him to sign some documents."

"That's good. After Finn left I began to get worried."

"Did Finn say anything else?"

"No, although he seemed to really want to speak to him, so I said I'd keep an eye out for him. I promised to call when he shows up."

"That's great and thank you. The papers he needs to sign are important."

Jennifer's number was called, and I pulled Cody to the side, where we wouldn't be overheard. "What do you think? Will he be coming back, or was he on his way somewhere else completely when he was arrested in Homer?"

"Hard to say. If he took all his stuff with him I'd lean toward him not planning to return. If he only took a few things north with him maybe he did plan to come back. At this point I don't suppose it matters. He'll either show up or he won't. If he doesn't, and Alex and Willow aren't successful in tracking him down, I guess we'll have to see if we can pick up another clue to where he's heading."

"Yeah. Maybe if he was in town for several weeks before he headed north he told someone what he was up to. We might want to ask around just in case."

"It couldn't hurt. I think we might be called next. Let's work our way to the front of the pack. I'd hate to miss our call and lose the table. I'm starving."

"Yeah, me too. Did we ever eat lunch?"

"Actually, we never did."

We were lucky enough to score an intimate table near the fireplace. Cody ordered lasagna and I went with the scallops and linguini. We both had a salad first and decided to share a bottle of wine. The restaurant was packed, but somehow, I felt like we were in our own little corner of the world.

"What did you think of Jennifer's suggestion of reserving a block of rooms at the inn for our wedding?" I asked. "I hadn't even considered we might have a lot of out-of-town family and friends to find lodging for. We'd need to give her plenty of notice for that to work."

"Yeah, about that," Cody said, a hitch of hesitation in his voice. "My mom called me yesterday to discuss the wedding. It seems my grandfather's health is declining, so she wanted to know if we'd consider traveling to Florida and having the wedding there."

"Florida?"

"I know it doesn't make sense. Your family and our friends are here. I wanted to tell her no, but she made me promise to at least discuss it with you."

I frowned. "I know I was the one who started this conversation by bringing up Jennifer's suggestion, but I'm feeling overwhelmed again. We were going to wait to make any plans until after the New Year. I think we should stick with that."

"It was a good plan, and I'm fine with waiting to discuss the specifics."

"But…?" I asked. "I can tell by your voice that there's a *but* you haven't mentioned yet."

"It's just that my mom pointed out that if we do get married in Florida we should do it in the winter so it won't be so hot. And the winter is the prime season in Florida, so we shouldn't wait to reserve a venue."

"So your mom wants us to get married in Florida next winter?"

"She wants us to get married in Florida *this* winter."

I was sure I should say something, but I found I was speechless. For a moment. And then panic set in. "This winter?" I screeched.

"I know we didn't want to hurry things, but I have a hard time saying no to my mother, so when she made me promise to at least talk to you about it I said I would. Now I can tell her we talked about it and you were against the idea and we can go back to our original plan."

I sat back with my mouth hanging open. "You aren't seriously sitting here telling me that you're afraid to say no to your mother, so you're willing to throw me under the bus by telling her I was the one who said no to her plan."

"Your voice is getting kind of loud," Cody whispered.

I was within two seconds of getting up and leaving when he put his hand over mine. He must have realized I'd become a flight risk because he squeezed my hand just a bit tighter than he really needed to. "I'm sorry. You have every right to be mad. I did plan to make you the bad guy and that was cowardly. I'll just tell my mom we're taking things slowly and we'll let her know what our plans are when we get around to making them."

I took a deep breath, then let it out. "Thank you. And I'm sorry about your grandfather. I guess it's reasonable for your mom to worry about his ability to travel. Maybe we can figure out a way to include him in our plans even if we have the wedding on the island. Perhaps we could have a second small reception in Florida for those who were unable to make the trip west."

Cody smiled. "That's a great idea. I should have thought of that myself."

"You probably would have if you weren't so busy planning to feed me to the wolves," I said, way too sweetly.

"Touché. Again, I'm sorry. I know I can come off as a tough guy, but my mom has a way of making me feel like I'm still five years old. She tells me to do something and I can't seem to say no, even if it's something I don't want to do."

"Your mom has a strong personality and she isn't afraid to wield her power to get what she wants. I might have panicked as well if I'd been the one talking to her. I'm sure my mom will have ideas we hate as well. It's important that we remember this is our wedding and we take our time to make sure it reflects our needs and desires."

"Maybe we should just elope," Cody said.

"Sounding better and better."

Chapter 9

Sunday, December 17

The conversation Cody and I had had the previous evening had left me feeling anxious, so I'd had a hard time sleeping. I kept imagining the broken relationships we'd leave spread across the battlefield if our mothers got into a tug-of-war over where we had the wedding, when, and who would be invited. I'd always dreamed of a big wedding with my family and friends in attendance, but just the hint of dissention had me seriously considering a quick trip to Vegas as a reasonable alternative.

By the time I'd downed my third cup of coffee, showered, and dressed for church, I was feeling much better. Cody would be by to get me in less than half an hour, so I didn't have a lot of time to spare, but I wanted to check in with Siobhan to make sure she didn't need any help wrapping things up at the house she and Finn were selling.

When I entered Maggie's kitchen through the back door, I found my sister and aunt sitting at the dining table sipping coffee. "Where is everyone?" I asked.

"Aiden's sleeping in, Danny never came home last night, Mom and Cassie went to early Mass, and Finn is in the shower," Siobhan filled me in.

I walked over to the coffeemaker and poured my own cup. "Cody's picking me up soon, but I wanted to ask if you and Finn needed any help at the house before I left. I know you said you have to be out this weekend."

Siobhan smiled. "We're completely finished. We moved the last of the boxes into storage yesterday before we had to leave for the sheriff's dinner and Finn hired a service to do the cleaning. I'm exhausted, he's exhausted, and we may very well be living with Maggie for quite some time, but we're out of the old house and ready to get on with the next phase of our lives."

"Good. I'm happy for you. I was worried this move would be tough on you and the baby. I meant to check in with you yesterday, but things got away from me."

"It does seem like you and Cody have taken on more than your fair share of projects," Maggie commented. "First there was Willow and her missing baby daddy and then I found out Cody was helping Jack Forrester with his housing project."

"It's not that he wants to help him; it's that Cody wants to help Burt get his house back, which means helping Jack, which now entails helping reunite Olivia with her daughter."

Siobhan laughed. "When you guys jump into a project you jump in with both feet."

"The original project to help the homeless people living in the warehouse get a new lease on life has turned into a complex and difficult undertaking. But I think everything we're doing is worthwhile."

Maggie squeezed my hand. "Everything you're doing is very worthwhile and I'm proud of you both. Cody explained his plan to get the council onboard with the housing project and I have to say I think it may just work. My feeling is that the council members who came out against the variance would like to see affordable housing; they just don't want to set a precedent they'll come to regret. Allocating land for a park to offset the denser land coverage on the adjoining tract seems like a stroke of genius."

"That's my fiancé." I smiled with pride. "A genius."

"You got a good one," Siobhan joined in. "We both did."

"Yes, we did. We just need to find Olivia's daughter and convince her to reconnect with her mother and we'll have something concrete to propose to the council."

"Have you heard from Willow?" Siobhan asked.

"Not yet, but they weren't heading up north until early this morning. I figured I'll call them if they don't call me by this evening. It would be so nice to get all these projects buttoned up in time to really enjoy the holidays." I glanced at the clock on the wall. "I should get going."

"We're all having dinner here if you and Cody can make it," Maggie informed me.

"I'd like that. I'll check with him, but go ahead and count us in."

Cody was just pulling into the drive when I arrived at my cabin. I told him I needed a minute to grab my things and I'd join him in his truck. I was especially looking forward to Mass today because the children's choir had been working so hard on a selection of Christmas carols I thought blended together to create a feeling of awe and reverence for the season.

"Maggie invited us to dinner," I said before I got busy and forgot to pass the news along.

"Sounds good. It's been a while since your whole family was together for Sunday dinner. Did Finn and Siobhan get moved out?"

"They did. At this point it looks like the house they were buying is definitely going to fall out of escrow, but they seem comfortable at Maggie's, so I imagine they'll be fine until they find something else. Is Burt okay at Mr. Parsons's house?"

"The two of them are getting along fine, but I can tell Burt would like to regain his independence. I made a few calls and ran a Google search, but so far I haven't been able to get a lead on where Rosemary might have gone after she left the island."

"I didn't know her well, but I do remember her. She's a few years older than me, I think around Aiden's age. She grew up on the island and attended school in Harthaven, so I'm sure she had friends who are still around. Maybe she kept in touch with a few. In fact, now that I think about it, I kind of remember she was good friends with Alyson Kilroy. If I see her at Mass I'll ask her if she knows where Rosemary ended up, or at least where she went when she first left Madrona."

Cody pulled into the church parking lot. It was already full, so we had to find a spot at the back. I noticed Father Kilian's koi pond was frozen over and his garden covered with snow. I wondered if Father Bartholomew would maintain them the way Father Kilian had. It would be a shame if they ended up being neglected. Of course, Sister Mary was still at the church, with no plans to leave St. Patrick's in the near future, so I was sure if Father Bartholomew didn't have a green thumb she'd take over the care of the garden.

"Alyson usually attends eleven o'clock Mass, so I'm going to look for her, if you don't mind getting the kids organized to go on," I said to Cody.

"That's fine. I'll meet you in the choir room."

The Mass that had been held before the eleven o'clock service had let out more than an hour before, but there were still people lingering in the hallway as they caught up with their friends and neighbors. The first arrivals for the eleven o'clock service had already begun to arrive but so far, I didn't see Alyson. I hoped if I just hung out near the entrance I could catch her as she came in. I was afraid if I waited until after Mass to look for her I'd miss her altogether. I didn't know her well enough to have her address or phone number, so catching her now was my best bet.

"No choir today?" Tara asked when she arrived with Parker and Amy.

"Yes, there is; Cody's getting the kids ready. I'm looking for Alyson Kilroy."

"I just saw her in the parking lot. She's heading this way."

"Great. Oh, Maggie's having dinner today if you'd like to come by. I think most of the family will be there."

Tara glanced at Parker.

"It's fine with me," he answered.

"Then we'd love to come, if you're sure it's okay with Maggie."

"She considers you family. I think Father Kilian and Sister Mary and probably Marley will be there as well. It's been a while since we had everyone for Sunday dinner."

"It has, and I'm looking forward to it."

"There's Alyson now. I'll catch up with you after the service."

I quickly texted Maggie to let her know that Tara, Parker, and Amy would be joining us for dinner and then headed toward the entrance to greet Alyson.

"Alyson," I called as she walked in through the front door.

"Oh, hi, Cait. Won't there be a choir today?"

"There is, but I hoped I could talk to you for a minute."

"Sure. What's up?"

"Let's go down the hall where we won't be in the way."

As soon as we were free of the crowd I turned and looked at her.

"Is everything okay?" she asked, concern on her face.

"Everything's fine. It's just that Cody and I are helping Olivia Stanwell track down Rosemary. I remembered you were friends and hoped you knew where she is."

Alyson frowned. "Olivia wants to find Rosemary? Why, after all these years?"

"She said time has given her perspective and she realizes she was wrong. She regrets the way things went and very much wants to reconcile with her daughter and meet her granddaughter."

Alyson paused, considering my words. "Are you sure Olivia doesn't have some ulterior motive for tracking Rosemary down?"

"I can't say I know what's in her heart, but Cody seemed to feel she was honest about looking to make amends and reconnect with her only child."

Alyson bit her lip, taking a moment before answering. "It crushed Rosemary when her mother bailed on her when she needed her the most. I wouldn't want to do anything that might cause her additional pain. Still, if Olivia's truly sorry and really is ready to apologize, Rosemary might be open to that."

"So you know where she is?" I asked.

"When she left here she went to stay with a friend in Portland. After her daughter, Hillary, was born she moved to Seattle to take a job working for one of the local television stations. I'm afraid we lost touch four or five years ago, but she might still be in touch with Grayson Hardwater."

Grayson had gone to school with Aiden and, again, though I didn't know him well, I was aware he'd left Madrona Island after they graduated. "Is he still living on Orcas Island?"

"As far as I know. He owns a hardware store, or at least he did at one point. Not a lot of people know this, but Grayson is Hillary's father. He and Rosemary hadn't been dating for more than a few weeks when she got pregnant. She didn't love him and didn't want to marry him, but she wanted him to be part of their child's life if he wanted to be. I know that, at least initially, she stayed in touch with him. He may know where she is now, but be warned, he has a wife and two children now. I don't know if they know about Rosemary and Hillary, so you might not want to ask him about her if there's anyone else around."

"Okay. Thanks. Maybe I'll head over to Orcas tomorrow and visit the hardware store. Don't worry, I'll be discreet. I wouldn't want to cause problems for him."

I headed to the choir room to join Cody and the kids, my mind on Grayson. I really hoped he knew where Rosemary was and would be willing to put me in touch with her. It would be nice to have at least one item on our ever-growing list of things to do checked off before we became mired in the obligations we had in the upcoming week.

******

Dinner at Maggie's was a lot of fun. Prior to the family home I grew up in burning down, Mom cooked a big dinner for the extended family almost every week. I admit I sometimes found the weekly dinners an obligation I resented, though now that she'd moved into a condo and the weekly gatherings had come to an end, I found I missed them.

Dinner this week had been informational as well as interesting. Father Kilian had announced he was formally leaving the priesthood after the first of the year and he and Maggie would marry next fall. I couldn't imagine waiting more than forty years to finally marry someone you'd known since high school was your soul mate. Neither of them had ever let on how they still felt about each other, though, looking back, I realized there were signs if only one had known to look for them.

My mother also announced she'd decided to take an extended vacation with the newish man in her life, Gabe Williams. Gabe's wife had passed away only eighteen months before he and my mother first met, so they'd been taking things slowly, but if the glances they shared were any indication I'd say things were about to heat up. I was happy Mom had found someone to love, especially because Cassie would be leaving home for college in less than a year. I had a feeling Cody and I would need to work our own wedding plans around both Maggie and Mom's, but given my joy in both these relationships I was thrilled to share my wedding year with them.

Not to be outdone by these announcements, Finn and Siobhan told us her baby was a boy and they were going to name him Connor. I couldn't wait for my nephew's arrival in June.

After dinner Cody and I went back to my cabin to spend some time alone before the demands of the week descended on us. We were trying to decide between watching a movie and wrapping presents when my phone rang. I looked at the caller ID before I answered.

"Hey, Alex. Did you make it to Homer okay?"

"We're here and checked in at the hotel."

"Anything to report?" I asked.

"Not yet. We spoke to the receptionist at the jail, who confirmed Bryce Barrington had spent time with them last week but has been released. She didn't know where he's gone and even if she did she wouldn't be at liberty to say. We checked a few hotels with no luck. Willow is pretty tired, so we're going to get some dinner and turn in early. We'll have all day tomorrow to look around. The pilot I hired isn't coming back for us until six o'clock."

"I ran into the woman who owns an inn here. She told me Bryce rented a room from her for the entire month. We're hoping if you don't find him in Homer he'll turn up here."

"That's good to know. I'll tell Willow. I can see the stress of trying to find him so she can put the baby up for adoption is putting a lot of pressure on her. Knowing that there's another lead should help."

"How's Harley?" I asked.

"He's fine. He didn't mind the flight at all, but he has a fit every time Willow and I try to separate. We started off with two hotel rooms, but the cat wouldn't settle down unless we were together, so we traded the rooms for a minisuite. Willow has the bedroom and I'll sleep on the foldout sofa."

"The cats Tansy sends are very intuitive. It could be Harley senses some sort of danger and doesn't want Willow to be alone. If he wants you in the same room I think it's a good idea you made the change."

"It sounds like Willow is out of the shower. I want to get some food in her, so I'm going to sign off. I'll call you again tomorrow."

"Okay. Have a nice evening, and don't let Willow overdo it."

I hung up and returned my attention to Cody, who was surfing through movie selections.

"Everything okay?" he asked.

"So far. Harley gets upset every time Willow is left alone, which concerns me a bit. You don't think she could be in some sort of danger, do you?"

"I don't see why she would be, unless she lied to us about the reason she's trying to track down Bryce Barrington."

"Do you think she might have lied? Could there be more going on than we know?"

Cody pulled me down onto the sofa next to him. "I hope not. Alex is with her, though, and I'm sure he'll keep her safe."

"I guess you're right. He seems to have accepted the role of knight in shining armor. I'm sure everything will be fine."

Cody pointed the remote at the television. "Drama or romance?"

"Romance, of course. The sappier the better."

Chapter 10

Monday, December 18

I set off for Orcas Island on the midmorning ferry. Cody had a newspaper to put out, but Coffee Cat Books was closed, so I had some time before we had to be at play rehearsal that evening. I had to admit I was beginning to get a little nervous about the play. The kids were great and seemed to be having a lot of fun, but most of them still didn't know their lines and there were only three rehearsals before the big night on Saturday. It wouldn't be the end of the world even if every child forgot their lines, and I remembered being nervous last year and a disastrous dress rehearsal. I'd been certain if the dress rehearsal wasn't perfect the play would be complete chaos, but in the end everything had worked out and I'd worried for nothing.

The short ferry ride was pleasant enough. There were snow flurries in the air, which lent atmosphere to the trip, and the interior of the large vessel was warm, so I sat down at a table on which I found one of the communal jigsaw puzzles provided for the passengers. I worked on a corner as I sipped the coffee I'd bought on the food deck. Even though riding a ferry was part of everyday life when you lived in the San Juan Islands, it was one I rather enjoyed most of the time. Not only was it warm and quiet, but the hum of the engines had a way of lulling me almost to sleep. The past week had been filled with ups and downs and it was nice to sit and work on a puzzle for a half hour.

My stomach fluttered as I thought about my errand today. Would Grayson be willing to speak to me? Would he be angry that I was clearly meddling in something he might very well wish he could forget had ever happened? Would he even know where Rosemary was, and if he did, would he be willing to share the information with someone he barely knew?

I realized focusing on the what-ifs wasn't going to help me in the least, so instead I decided to focus on a phone call I'd received from Balthazar Pottage that morning. As promised, he'd spoken to his business manager, who'd been able to dig up jobs and housing for Sam and Isabelle. Both had appointments with him tomorrow morning, so I'd asked Danny if he'd be willing to drive them into Seattle. He was happy to do it, although he didn't have a vehicle large enough to transport Sam's whole family, so I'd asked Father Bartholomew if we could borrow the church van, which sat fifteen. He'd agreed, and the whole group had left on the ferry that departed Madrona Island just ahead of the one I was on.

Cody had given them cash for food and a room for tonight, plus enough to get by until Sam and Isabelle earned their first paycheck. Danny would stay with them until he was sure everything went well. When they were settled he'd come home on the next ferry leaving Anacortes for Madrona Island. If Sam and Isabelle met with Balthazar's manager tomorrow morning Danny should be able to make the last ferry tomorrow.

It felt good to have accomplished what we'd set out to do with Sam and Isabelle. Now if we could just find Bryce for Willow and figure out a way to convince Rosemary to come home for Christmas, we'd be batting a thousand. It would be nice to be able to sit back and enjoy the holiday knowing we'd managed to help everyone.

As soon as the ferry docked on Orcas Island, I made my way to the hardware store. I hoped Grayson hadn't moved on from there because I didn't have any other leads and Christmas was only a week away. I wondered if Olivia would still donate the property if we managed to put her in touch with Rosemary but we weren't able to do it before Christmas. Knowing Olivia, probably not.

It was still snowing lightly, but the parking area near the hardware store was empty, so I parked as close to the front of the building as possible and hurried inside. I wasn't sure Grayson would know who I was, but I was sure he'd remember Aiden, so I decided to introduce myself as his sister.

"Can I help you?" the man behind the counter asked.

"Are you Grayson Hardwater?"

"I am. And who might you be?"

"I'm Caitlin Hart, Aiden Hart's little sister."

He smiled. "Of course. I thought you looked familiar. How can I help you today?"

I looked around the store. There were no customers, so I jumped right in. "I'm trying to get in touch with Rosemary Stanwell and was told you might know where I could find her."

I could see Grayson was both surprised and concerned by my request.

"Why do you want to get ahold of Rosemary?" he asked.

I took a deep breath and dove in. "I'm looking for her on behalf of her mother. I guess you probably know Olivia and Rosemary had a falling out when Olivia found out she was pregnant. My fiancé, Cody West, recently spoke with Olivia, and during that conversation, she expressed remorse for the way things worked out. She'd very much like to reconcile with her daughter and meet her granddaughter, so Cody and I are trying to help get them together."

He drummed his fingers on the counter but didn't answer right away. I could tell by the series of expressions crossing his face that he was trying to figure out how to handle the situation. I didn't blame him. If I was the one who knew where Rosemary was, I'm not sure I'd give the information to some random person I barely knew.

After a minute Grayson spoke. "Are you certain it's Mrs. Stanwell's intention to reconcile with Rosemary? That this whole thing isn't just some elaborate attempt to get her to come home for some other reason?"

"What other reason could there be?"

"I don't know. What I do know is that I don't trust her mother not to hurt Rosemary again."

Grayson had a point. I'd never even spoken to Olivia, and the only proof Cody had that Olivia really wanted to make amends with her daughter was her word. "I guess Olivia hurt Rosemary pretty bad."

"She crushed her. When Rosemary found out she was pregnant she was scared stiff. She was young and confused and needed the support her mother could have provided. Instead, Olivia gave her an ultimatum: Give the baby up for adoption or raise the baby on her own. Rosemary was terrified to be on her own, but she very much wanted to keep the baby. She's doing well now, but those first years were very hard for her. To be honest, I'm not sure she'll even want to speak to her mother."

"I'd considered that," I said. "But I also considered the fact that she may actually welcome the chance for her daughter to meet and have a relationship with her grandmother. It's been ten years. Both women are different people now."

Grayson bowed his head. "True. It would be nice for Hillary to have a relationship with at least one of her grandparents."

"So you'll help me?"

"I don't feel comfortable giving you Rosemary's address or phone number, but I'll tell her you're looking for her and that her mother would like to see her."

I jotted down my cell number on a piece of paper. "That sounds fair. Please ask her to call me if she has any questions."

"I will. And for the record, I think it's nice that you're trying to help them reconnect."

I'd turned to leave when Grayson spoke again. "You'll keep this to yourself, won't you?"

I turned back around. "You never told your wife about Hillary?"

Grayson shook his head. "I'm afraid I let things get a lot more complicated than they should have been. When Rosemary told me she was pregnant I panicked. I didn't believe what she was telling me. We were only together that one time and barely knew each other."

"You weren't dating?"

"No. We hooked up at a party. It was all very spontaneous and we regretted it immediately. She didn't love me and I didn't love her. In fact, I was in love with someone else who'd recently broken up with me, which is partly why I was at the party in the first place."

"So you never saw each other again after that?"

"We'd run into each other around town, but no, we never dated or even explored a friendship. By the time Rosemary told me that night had resulted in a child, I was back with the girl I loved. We're married now. I was scared she'd break up with me again if she found out I was with someone else during our brief time apart, so I never said a thing."

"Do you regret not knowing your daughter?"

"At times. When Rosemary first told me about the pregnancy I panicked. I was sure keeping the whole thing a secret was the only option. But there are times I wonder what might have been if I'd made an effort to have a relationship with Rosemary's daughter. I didn't have the emotional maturity I needed to think clearly then."

"So Hillary isn't in your life at all?"

"Not really. When Rosemary told me she wanted to keep the baby I was scared about what that would mean for my life. I told her I supported her decision to do what she felt was right for her, but I also said it was important to me that no one know I was her baby's father. She said she was fine with that; she thought of the baby as hers, not ours, anyway. I sent her money to help out when I could, but eventually Rosemary got a job making a lot more than I did, and she told me that she didn't want anything more. Rosemary sends me a photo every now and again, but that's the extent of it. We agreed to stay in touch just in case Hillary needed something in the future that only I could provide."

"That was a smart decision. You never know when your child might need bone marrow or a kidney."

"Exactly. In that event I'd be there for her, no matter what."

I thanked Grayson for sharing what he had and headed back to the ferry. On the ride back I asked myself if I'd want to know if Cody had fathered a child I didn't know about. Part of me felt it would be better to live my life in ignorant bliss, but another part was certain that, in the end, I'd want to know. I didn't think Cody and I had any secrets. At least not anything big, like the one Grayson was living with. Cody had been out of my life completely for ten years. A lot can happen in ten years. Still, even though we hadn't been together then, Cody was still

Cody. There was no way he would ever turn his back on a child of his no matter what he had to risk.

******

After I returned to Madrona Island I popped into the newspaper office to see if Cody wanted to grab a bite. It was late for lunch, but I hadn't eaten and suspected he hadn't either.

"I'm starving," Cody said. "Is the Driftwood okay? It's close and I have some work to finish up before I can quit for the day."

"The Driftwood is fine."

Cody grabbed his jacket and locked the door behind us. We walked down the street hand in hand despite the bracing cold.

"How did things go with Grayson?" Cody asked.

"He knows how to get in touch with Rosemary but didn't feel comfortable giving me her contact info. He took my number and promised to pass it along to Rosemary, along with the information that her mother would really like to see her."

"Did he think she'd be interested in seeing her mother?"

"He wasn't sure. Olivia hurt Rosemary deeply at a time when she really needed her. Grayson said he wouldn't be surprised if she didn't want to have anything to do with her mother, but he felt it was possible she might want Hillary to get to know her grandmother, so maybe…"

"It's a sad situation. I wish we could do more, but things are in Rosemary's hands now; we've done what we can."

I opened the door to the café and we went inside, settling into a booth in the corner. "All in all, I'd say we had a good day. Danny's on his way to Seattle with Sam and Isabelle and a message will be getting to Rosemary. Now, if we can just track down the father of Willow's baby, our work will be done."

Cody waved at the waitress, indicating he'd like some coffee. "Have you heard from either Willow or Alex?"

"Not since last night. I imagine we'll hear from them before they board the plane to come home. I hope for Willow's sake—and the sake of mankind—that they're successful in their mission."

"Knowing what we do about the baby really does add a unique twist to the whole thing."

The waitress poured our coffee and took our orders. Once she'd left our conversation turned to plans for that evening.

"We're eating a late lunch, so why don't we grab dinner after play practice?" Cody suggested.

"Fine. Maybe we can do some shopping as well. I'm beginning to stress over how many gifts I still need to get."

"Not everything will be open, but we can hit the shops in Harthaven that stay open late. What we really need is a day to head to Seattle."

"I don't see that happening."

"What about mail order? If we get our orders in tonight and pay for expedited shipping, we should be all right."

"I like that idea. Maybe we should just pick up takeout after rehearsal. We can head back to my cabin, find what we need online, then snuggle up and watch it snow."

"Now that sounds like my kind of a plan."

Chapter 11

Thursday, December 21

"Gingerbread latte with an extra shot, peppermint hot cocoa with extra whip, and a white chocolate hot cocoa with no whip," Lucy Colter rattled off as I took her order at the coffee bar.

"Would you like any pastries with that?" I asked.

Lucy glanced at the selection behind the glass display case. "Throw in a couple of sugar cookies and a piece of ginger cake." She turned to look at the line of children that had formed near the front door waiting for Santa. "It looks like the kids are going to be a while. I'll just eat my cake and sip my latte while I wait."

"Our Santa likes to take his time with each child, which makes for longer lines but a much more satisfying experience than you get with most."

"My kids adored Alex when he was here two years ago. I was happy to see he'd come back. Interesting choice, having a pregnant elf, though."

I smiled as I looked at Willow, who was standing slightly behind Alex with her hand on his shoulder as he lifted a dark-haired girl onto his lap. "When we hired Willow it wasn't our intention that she be an elf, but she loves working with kids and she's really good at getting the perfect photo." It also seemed as if Willow had been enjoying spending as much time with Alex as possible since they'd been back from Alaska, but I didn't say as much.

Lucy handed me her credit card, which I ran after ringing up her order.

"Will you be attending the Christmas play at St. Patrick's this year?" I asked as I handed her card back. She was a Baptist, so she didn't attend St. Pat's, but a lot of the islanders who didn't attend the church came for the play anyway.

"The kids and I are planning to. My husband has to work that night, but he has Christmas off, so that's something."

"It must be hard being married to a firefighter. Someone has to be on shift even if it's a holiday."

"We always find a way to work around his schedule, but it'll be nice to have him home for both Christmas Eve and Christmas this year. I'm going to take my goodies and sit in the lounge. If the kids don't see me when they're done send them in."

"Okay. Enjoy the ginger cake."

I glanced at Willow, who was laughing at something Alex said. The pair had shown up for work as scheduled on Tuesday, and ever since then I'd been trying to figure out if there was more going on than simple friendship. They worked together all day and then, on both Tuesday and Wednesday after closing, they'd gone off to one holiday-themed event or another. They hadn't had any luck tracking Bryce down in Homer, which I would have thought would have upset Willow, but she'd seemed happier in the last couple of days than I'd seen her before. Not that I'd known her all that long, but still… She wasn't any closer to her goal, but she seemed to be handling it well.

"It looks like things are slowing down a bit if you want to take a break," Tara said. "Alex and Willow want to go to lunch at one and Cassie just got back."

"What about you?" I asked my hardworking best friend.

"I brought a sandwich, so I don't need a break."

"You *do* need a break and I'm going to insist you take one. Call Parker; maybe he can get away for a few minutes and you can meet him in the hospital cafeteria."

Tara hesitated.

"Take a break," I insisted. "If Parker can't meet you go shopping or bundle up and take a walk."

"I did want to look for a necklace for Amy for Christmas, and I want to find a really nice photo album for Sister Mary. I thought I'd make copies of my favorite photos from my childhood and give them to her."

"Oh my God, that's the sweetest thing I've ever heard. She'll love it."

"She mentioned during one of our lunches that one of the things she regretted the most about the way things unfolded was that she didn't have a lot of memories and keepsakes from my childhood. I'm hoping the photo album will help fill the void."

"It will. It's a sweet and thoughtful gift. Go do your shopping. I'm fine here with the others, so take as long as you need."

Tara hugged me. "Okay, thanks. I'll try not to be too long."

Tara had a way of figuring out the perfect gift for any person on any occasion, while I had a hard time coming up with anything more personal or creative than a sweater or piece of sporting equipment. Cody and I had managed to knock out our list with our mail-order marathon, but I still needed something for him and was totally clueless as to what to get the man who seemed to have everything he wanted and needed.

"Excuse me, miss." A young woman holding the hand of a blond-haired preschooler who looked to be three or maybe four walked up behind me.

"Yes, can I help you?"

"I'm interested in one of the kittens you have in the lounge. I understand they're available for adoption."

"To the right person. Which kitten are you interested in?"

"The fuzzy white one. Annabelle seems to have fallen in love with her."

"Do you live here on the island?" I asked.

"We just moved here two months ago. Annabelle loves animals, but until now we've lived in an apartment, so we haven't had the opportunity to let her have one."

I turned and looked at the child. "How old are you, Annabelle?"

"Five."

Older than I thought.

"Have you held a kitten before?"

"A couple of times. My cousins have cats."

"Okay. Let's go back to the lounge to see if you and Snow White like each other."

I told Cassie to keep an eye on the counter, then led the woman and her daughter back to the cat lounge. I had Annabelle sit on one of the sofas and gently put Snow White into her arms.

I was glad to see the little girl held the kitten firmly yet not too tight. Some younger kids held the cats so tightly it frightened them, but Annabelle didn't appear to be at all afraid of the animal and Snow White seemed content to allow the girl to hold her.

"There's an application that needs to be filled out if you're interested in adopting Snow White."

The woman glanced at her daughter. "Are you sure about this, Annabelle?"

"Oh, I am. Please, Mama?"

The mother looked at me. "I'll take an application."

I watched Annabelle with the kitten while her mother filled out the paperwork I gave her. She spoke softly to the kitten, who responded by purring loudly. Occasionally, I'm hesitant to place a kitten with such a young child, but in this case my instinct told me Snow White and Annabelle were going to be very happy together.

I glanced at the application the woman handed me. She lived with her husband and daughter in a three-bedroom house with a fenced yard. Her daughter went to Harthaven Elementary School, her husband worked for the local utility company, and the woman worked as a housekeeper for the Harthaven Inn.

"You work for Jennifer," I stated.

"I do. She's a very nice woman and so far, I've enjoyed my job quite a lot. Not only is Jennifer extremely easy to get along with, but she's been flexible with my hours, and the guests who stay at the Inn are very nice as well."

"It's a lovely place," I agreed. "There's a man who's been staying there named Bryce Barrington. Do you know him?"

"Sure, I know Bryce. Whenever I went in to clean his room he'd play me a song on his guitar. It was the highlight of my day, although he hasn't been there for more than a week."

"I need to speak to him about a fairly important matter. Do you happen to know if he's coming back?"

She hesitated.

"I don't mean to make you uncomfortable if you'd rather not say."

"You seem nice enough and I'm sure your business with Bryce is on the up-and-up. I don't know for certain what his plans are because he left without saying anything to me, but he did leave some of his belongings in his room, including his guitar, so my guess is that, yes, he'll return."

I smiled. "Great. I'll catch up with him when he gets back. As for the kitten, Snow White looks like she loves Annabelle, who appears to return the affection. Your application seems to be in order, so if you'd like to adopt the kitten I think we can proceed. I'll give you a list of items you'll need, including high-quality cat food, a cat bed, and a litter box. If you plan to travel with her you'll also need a cat carrier. We have a cardboard carrier you can use to get her home and to the veterinarian. Once you have everything together come on back and I'll load your new baby into your car."

"Speaking of the veterinarian, will she need shots? Can you recommend someone?"

"The kitten has had her first shots and you'll get a voucher to have the cat spayed. It's a good idea to establish a relationship with your vet right away. The packet I'll give you has the name and contact information of two. Both are excellent, so whichever is closer to where you live should be fine. I'll also give you my cell number in case you have any questions. We want you and Snow White to be happy."

She shook my hand. "Thank you. I think we'll love having Snow White as a part of our family."

After Annabelle and her mother left I headed back to the half of the building that housed the bookstore. There was still a long line to see Santa, but both Willow and Alex had huge smiles on their faces, so I thought they'd be fine until their lunch break at one. Based on the line that had already formed, I realized I'd have to cut the line off for the time being so we didn't end up with people waiting through Alex's break.

The fact that Bryce had left his guitar behind indicated to me that he did plan to return. Even though Willow had seemed fine since the trip to Homer, I figured she'd be relieved to hear it, so I pulled her aside and shared my news.

"That's great," she replied.

I couldn't help but notice her smile didn't quite reach her eyes. "You do still want to have him sign off on the adoption?"

"Of course. I know that allowing the Plimptons to adopt my son is the best thing for him. It's just that I've enjoyed being here on the island and at the store. I'll be sorry when my errand is over."

"Tara and I want you to stay for as long as you want. We need the help and we'd love it if you'd consider something longer term. At least until the baby's born."

Willow glanced at Alex. I couldn't help but notice the frown that crossed her face. "Can I think about it and let you know?"

"Absolutely. Take as much time as you need."

Cody called me a short time later to ask if I wanted to go to lunch. I told him I'd let Tara go, though I was hungry, and he offered to buy takeout to bring to the bookstore. Cassie could keep her eye on the front and we could eat in the office, and if a load of customers came in at once, we'd be there to help if necessary. The next ferry wasn't due until after two and I was pretty sure Tara would be back by then.

******

"They have new rolls at the deli," I commented a half hour later as Cody handed me a turkey sandwich on a parmesan-crusted roll.

"They still have the rolls they've always had, but they added three new flavors. I decided we should try two of them, so I got cracked pepper for myself."

"Did you finish the article you've been working on?"

"I have. And, even better, I heard from Olivia."

I was almost afraid to ask about the outcome, but Cody *had* said "even better." "And…?"

"And she told me that her daughter had called her and they spoke. Rosemary hasn't committed to coming for Christmas, but she was willing to think about it, so Olivia considers we've met our half of the deal and will be happy to donate the land for the park."

I grinned. "That's wonderful."

"Now I just need to present the package to the island council. If I can get them to go along with the plan Burt should be back in his house by New Year's."

"Will there even be a council meeting between now and New Year's?"

"No. But I've made appointments with each of the council members. Forrester has said that if I can get them to sign off on at least entertaining the concept he'll allow Burt back into his home, although he won't sign the deed back over to him until the deal is complete and everything has been signed."

I leaned forward and hugged Cody. "That's terrific. Have you told Burt?"

"No, and I'm not going to until I speak to the council members. I'm hoping by the end of the day tomorrow we'll at least have a verbal agreement to proceed with my idea."

"Do you want me to come with you to talk to everyone?"

"Actually," Cody said, "Siobhan has agreed to come with me. She has the respect of the entire council and I think they'll listen to her. My last appointment for today isn't until seven, so I'm afraid I'll have to cancel dinner."

"I'll make something. We can share a late meal when you get done and use the time to catch each other up on our day."

Cody leaned over and kissed me quickly on the lips. "Deal."

Chapter 12

I decided to call Grayson after Cody left to thank him for passing along my message. To be honest, I hadn't been sure he would. It was hard for me to understand how a parent could turn her back on her own child, but I guess I could imagine how difficult the situation had been for him. He hadn't been in love with Willow, had, in fact, been in love with another woman, and I found I could imagine how fear of losing her had played into his actions.

"Grayson, hi, it's Cait Hart."

"Cait. How are you?"

"I'm good. I just wanted to thank you for passing along my message. I heard Rosemary had called her mother and they'd had a pleasant conversation."

I listened as Grayson let out a breath. "I'm glad it worked out. When I spoke to Rosemary she seemed uncertain. I wasn't sure she would call. I'm glad she did."

"It's been ten years. I imagine both of them have changed in that time. Maybe they can work something out."

"Yeah. Maybe."

"You sound uncertain."

"It's not that," Grayson answered. "It's just that it's been years since I spoke to Rosemary. Calling her on your behalf gave me a reason to catch up with her, and we had a very nice conversation. She told me about Hillary's school play and the dance classes she loves so much. I know this might seem odd, considering I've never once met my daughter, but suddenly I realized I missed being part of her life."

"Do you think you'll try to see her?" I asked.

"I don't know. I wouldn't do it behind my wife's back. I feel like our relationship is really solid. A lot more solid that it was when I first found out I was going to be a father. Maybe the time has come to tell her."

"It's a risk for sure, but in the end it might be the best choice. Whatever you decide, your secret is safe with me and I wish you well."

I spoke to Grayson for a while longer before we hung up. There were times when the path before us appeared dark and uncertain. I hoped Grayson was able to find a way to incorporate all his children into his life.

******

"So, did you find the gifts you wanted to buy?" I asked Tara later that afternoon.

"I did. The necklace I found for Amy is exactly what I'd envisioned, and Maggie offered to make me

146

a patchwork cover for my photo album out of fabric we're going to harvest from a box of old clothes my mom gave me from when I was a kid."

"You have clothes from your childhood?"

"A few things. A few favorite dresses and the T-shirt I got when my parents took me to Disneyland. Stuff like that. I'm kind of surprised my mom kept them. She isn't really the sentimental sort."

"Are you sure you want to cut up your keepsakes?"

"Yes. I'm going to make three photo album covers from them: one for Sister Mary, one for my mom, and one for me. They'll be identical, with the same photos inside."

I loved the idea. "Christmas is in only a few days. Are you going to have enough time to make three photo albums?"

"I already bought the albums. I gave them, along with the bag of clothes, to Maggie. She and Marley are going to take care of making the covers, so all I have to do is pick out some photos and make three copies of each one."

"You're always so creative. I never know what to get for the people in my life."

"Oh, I don't know. I use the measuring cups you got me for Christmas last year all the time."

I frowned. "Are you making fun of my gift?"

"No. I'm really not. In fact, I was very touched that you remembered I shared with you that my half-cup measuring cup had melted in the dishwasher."

I still wasn't 100 percent certain Tara really had liked the gift or was teasing me, but I let it go. "Cody and I picked out gifts together this year, but I still have no idea what to get for him. You're so good at gift giving. Any suggestions?"

Tara twisted her lips to the side. "I have no idea what to get for Parker either. I feel like our relationship has gotten pretty serious, but we aren't engaged or anything, so I hate to get him anything too personal. But a shirt or sweater doesn't seem right either. What did you get Cody last year?"

"A shirt. But," I grinned, "instead of wrapping the shirt I wore it, and only it, to bed on Christmas Eve."

Tara laughed. "As creative as that sounds, Parker has Amy to consider, so I won't be spending the night on Christmas Eve."

"I guess having a child in the mix does complicate things. Speaking of which, I had an interesting conversation with Willow earlier."

"Interesting how?"

"I spoke to a woman this afternoon who works in housekeeping over at the Inn. I asked her about Bryce Barrington and she said he left some of his stuff in his room, including his guitar. That seemed to indicate to me that he planned to come back to Madrona Island. When I told Willow she said she was happy to hear it, but she didn't seem happy to me."

"You think she's beginning to change her mind about the adoption?" Tara asked.

"I don't know. She's seemed different since she got back from Alaska. I think she and Alex might have something going on."

"I've noticed that as well. I guess if they got together that wouldn't be a bad thing."

"Yeah, I guess." I thought about what Tansy had said about the baby being at a crossroads. One path would lead him to his intended destiny and the other wouldn't. When Willow told me about the wealthy couple she wanted to have adopt her baby I'd figured helping her make that happen was my task. Now I wasn't so certain. Alex had a lot of money and could provide a top-rate education for Willow's child too, but Tansy had made it sound like this was something that had only one right answer. "Just so you know," I added, "I asked Willow to stay. At least until the baby's born."

"And…?"

"And she said she'd think about it. I had the feeling she's uncertain about things with Alex but is interested enough to at least want to take him into consideration. Of course, I don't know what she's thinking. I've just formed some impressions based on her moods and behavior."

"I think I agree with you," Tara said. "It does seem as if Alex has become part of the equation. I wonder if he knows that, and if he does, how he feels about it."

Suddenly, it occurred to me things might have become a whole lot more complicated.

******

When Cody arrived with burgers and a frown later that evening I was pretty sure his day hadn't gone the way he hoped. "Bad news?"

Cody paused and tilted his head. He took a minute to place the burgers on the plates I'd set out before he answered. "I wouldn't necessarily say bad news," he responded as he bit into a french fry.

"Maybe you should explain." I took a sip of my wine and waited.

"Siobhan told me that to amend an ordinance, which is basically what we want to do, we need a three-quarters vote rather than a simple majority. There are five council members, so we can only have one *no* vote for the proposal to go through. At this point we have two council members who've verbally agreed to my idea, although both wanted specific language in the amendment. Siobhan thinks we can meet their needs. We also have Hank Tyson, who's on the fence. Of the two council members Siobhan and I plan to meet with tomorrow, she feels one will be a firm *yes* and one a firm *no*."

"So you have to convince Hank to vote for the amendment for it to pass."

"Exactly."

"Any ideas how to make sure he gets off the fence on your side?" I asked.

"Siobhan thinks Hank can be swayed if offered the right incentive. He's an elected official, so we can't bribe him. According to her, he's a reasonable man, so we'll need to sway him using logic and intellect, not just emotion, or some combination of the tools available to us. I already tried the argument that the project would be good for the community, but that didn't seem to do the trick. We'll need to think of something else."

I picked up my napkin and wiped a drop of ketchup from my mouth. "What if we made it personal?" I asked. "We know there are quite a few young couples on the island who were born and grew up here and would like to stay and raise their own children here, but they're looking at a reality where they'll have to choose between home ownership and staying. What if we got together a group of people who would benefit from this amendment and let them plead their case directly to Hank and the other council members?"

"That isn't a bad idea. I don't see how we can do something like that until after the New Year, but maybe we could put Hank into contact with two or three couples who fit the demographic we're trying to help. Perhaps we could take Hank to lunch."

"We'll need to do it tomorrow with Christmas next week."

"Do you know any couples who might be available on such short notice?"

"I can come up with a few. You call Hank and ask him about lunch. I'll call Siobhan and we'll brainstorm the best couples to ask."

Fortunately, Siobhan thought of some couples immediately and even agreed to call them as the mayor to ask if they'd be free for a couple of hours the next day. I could hear Cody on the phone with Hank, so I asked Siobhan to call me back with a time and place, then headed out onto the deck to let Max run around for a few minutes. It was beautiful when the beach was covered with snow and the clouds had cleared. The reflection of the moon on the sea was just about the most awe-inspiring sight I'd ever seen.

I was about to call Max back to go inside when my phone rang.

"Hey, Tara, what's up?"

"Willow got a call from the Plimptons. Apparently, they've thought things over and have decided not to require the father's signature given Willow's situation. They want to proceed with the adoption whether he's found or not."

I wasn't sure whether to be relieved or concerned. "How did Willow take the news?"

"I'm not sure. She said she was relieved, but she didn't look that way. I asked her if she was still planning to remain on the island, and she said she wasn't sure. She told me she was tired and headed into her room with Harley. I'm pretty sure I heard her crying. I don't know what to do."

"Don't do anything," I recommended. "I need to call Tansy to see if she can tell me anything more. I'll come into work early tomorrow and we can talk more then."

"I've been expecting your call," Tansy greeted me when she picked up her phone.

"You know the potential adoptive parents have waived their requirement of the father's signature?"

"I do."

"And...?" I asked. "Is this good news or bad? When you first told me about the baby and that he needed to be raised in an affluent family I was sure the reason Harley was here was to make certain we found the baby daddy. I suppose that might still be true, but somewhere along the way Willow and Alex Turner became friends, and it's possible their friendship could turn into something more. Both Alex and the Plimptons can provide Willow's baby with a top-notch education. I guess my question is, does it really matter which path the child takes?"

Tansy seemed to hesitate. I hated that she seemed uncertain. I'd always been able to count on her being sure.

"I believe it does matter," Tansy answered. "Having the ability to financially provide the education the child needs is only part of the equation.

My sense is that there are other opportunities that will mold the boy's future that exist on only one of the paths open to him."

"Okay, so then do you know which path we need to steer him toward?"

Tansy took a breath. "No. I wish I could say I have a clear sense, but I don't. All I really know is that the child is at a crossroads. One path will lead him to his destiny and the other won't."

I suppressed the urge to scream in frustration. "Okay. Help me out here. Willow no longer needs the father's signature to continue with the adoption. For all I know, she might be thinking of leaving the island tomorrow. Do I allow her to leave or do I stop her? Do I support her plan to give the baby up for adoption or do I try to convince her to wait to make a final decision, thereby giving her time to work out her relationship with Alex?"

"My best advice is to follow the cat."

Of course. I had almost forgotten about Harley and his role in all of this. Not only had Harley gone to Alaska with Willow and Alex, but after they'd returned Willow had taken Harley back to Tara's with her. There was no doubt in my mind that Willow and the cat were linked. All I needed to do was watch the cat and try to support whatever action he made.

I thanked Tansy and hung up. Then I called to Max, who was busy chasing the waves.

"Aren't you cold out here?" Cody asked when he joined me on the deck.

"I was just coming in. Did you work out a lunch with Hank?"

"Sort of. Siobhan and Hank are going to meet with three couples. He didn't want to do lunch, so they're getting together in Siobhan's office. She didn't think I should be there, so she's going to call me afterward to let me know how it went."

Max joined us and we went into the cabin. "Siobhan is very persuasive. I think this could work."

"I agree," Cody said. "Did I hear you talking to someone before I joined you on the deck?"

I explained that the Plimptons had waived their requirement and filled him in on my conversation with Tansy.

"It's somewhat alarming that Tansy isn't getting a clear reading," Cody said. "I feel like we're being asked to manipulate the lives of Willow and her child without having a firm grasp on the situation."

"I'm not loving it either. I suppose there wouldn't be any harm in trying to convince Willow to stay here at least through Christmas. As far as we know, she doesn't have anywhere else to go, and it would give us longer to figure things out. I hate to jump in on one side or the other until we know more."

"Agreed."

"There is one thing that occurred to me as I spoke to Tansy, though: regardless of whether Willow needs his signature, Bryce is the baby's father. He has the right to know of his existence."

Cody nodded.

"It's my opinion we should continue to look for him."

"So where do we start?"

"In the past week or so we've tracked him from Madrona Island to Homer, Alaska. I'm wondering why he went to Alaska when he had a prepaid room for an entire month here. Once he arrived in Alaska he was involved in a bar fight that ended with a stint in jail. What was he fighting about and who was he fighting with? And he's been out of jail for a week, yet he hasn't shown up back on Madrona despite having a room and possessions waiting for him. Willow and Alex didn't find him in Alaska. Where is he?"

"That's a lot of questions."

"It is. And I have no idea what to do next."

Cody leaned over and kissed me on the lips. "We'll figure it out."

I smiled. "I know we will. We always do. Siobhan's going to be busy with Hank tomorrow, so we should see Finn. Maybe he can help us find at least some of the answers. I need to go into the bookstore and I promised I'd come in early, but maybe we can have Finn come by once the rush from the first ferry clears out."

"That sounds like a good plan. In the meantime, I'll do a search to see if I can figure out what Bryce might have been up to in Homer. It's a good possibility he's still there even though Willow and Alex didn't find him."

Cody was going back to Mr. Parsons's tonight, so we said our good-byes and I went up to bed. I rested my back against a mound of pillows and looked out the window at the calm sea. Knowing the outcome of this latest task had such huge implications for mankind was making me uncomfortable. Tansy didn't seem to have a clear read on things, which was a departure from the norm, but somehow I knew it was my own intuition I'd need to trust as we navigated the next few days.

Chapter 13

Friday, December 22

I arrived at Coffee Cat Books sixty minutes before opening. The tree was already lit, carols were playing, and a fire was dancing in the fireplace. Tara was busy setting up the coffee bar, so I got the cats settled in the cat lounge, then jumped in to restock shelves while we talked.

"How was Willow this morning?" I asked.

Tara added paper cups to the stack in front of her before answering. "It was obvious she'd been crying, but she joined me for breakfast and I could see she was at least attempting to put on a happy face."

"Did she happen to mention what her plans might be?"

Tara broke down the box she'd just emptied and set it aside. "Yes, she did. She told me that she'd thought long and hard about the situation. On one hand, if there was no longer a requirement of obtaining Bryce's signature on the adoption form she didn't have a reason to stay on the island, but she'd made a commitment to us to help out through the holidays that she very much wanted to keep."

"That's good. I feel it's important she stay at least for now."

"I agree. I reminded her that we wanted her to stay until after the baby was born. I pointed out that she had a secure job with us and a safe place to stay, and she agreed to think about it. She asked if I knew Alex's plans and I answered honestly that I wasn't sure what he'd be doing after the holidays. She tried to make it sound like she was just asking in passing, but I could tell there was more going on in her mind than she wanted to share."

I stacked the books in my arms on the shelf. "I feel so sorry for her. All the uncertainty must be really difficult to deal with."

"Yeah, she's in a tough spot."

"Did she say where she stood on her search for Bryce?" I wondered.

"We talked about that and agreed that even though the Plimptons weren't insisting on his signature anymore, Bryce deserved to know he was going to be a father. She had no idea how to continue the search, other than to hope he came back to Madrona on his own, but if new leads turned up she wanted to follow them."

"That's good. Cody and I feel the same way. We're meeting with Finn later to try to come up with a strategy. Something must have happened in the past couple of weeks that made Bryce change his plans. Jennifer told me he paid cash for a room at the Inn for an entire month. Why would he do that if he planned to head to Alaska? Why not just rent the room for the nights he needed it? I don't think the trip north was planned."

"It does seem like there may be something going on."

"The other part of the puzzle is that Bryce was at the Inn during the time Willow was looking for him. Sure, she was looking for a man named Trace and she didn't have a last name or a photo, but this is a small island. If she was here for more than a month asking around about him don't you think he would have heard?"

"You think he was intentionally avoiding her?"

I shrugged. "I don't know, but it seems unlikely Willow could be asking everyone about him without him finding out she was here. I hope he didn't take off for Alaska because he spotted her and didn't want to deal with the situation."

"He might not know the baby is his even if he did see her," Tara pointed out.

"True, but he would at least suspect."

Tara glanced toward the door. "It looks like Willow, Alex, and Harley are on their way, so maybe we should change the topic."

"Did you ever order any more peppermint syrup?" I asked immediately.

"I did, and it should be with the shipment we still need to unpack. I want to run a special on peppermint-flavored drinks for the next two days because tomorrow will be the last day we'll be open until after Christmas. I want to use up the entire inventory."

I paused. "Wow. I hadn't even thought about the fact that we only have two more sales days before Christmas. I feel like the holiday has really snuck up on me."

"Doesn't it always?"

I grabbed a new box of inventory from the pile. "Yeah, I guess it does."

I watched Willow and Alex as they entered the store. They were both smiling as Alex set Harley on the Santa chair and Willow placed her elf cap on her head. Alex asked if they could help us prepare for opening, so Tara had him bring the last of the boxes in from the back.

"How are you feeling today?" I asked Willow.

"Good. I had a bit of a rough night, but I think I've sorted things out in my head and I find I'm excited for whatever the future brings."

I smiled. "That's great. Tara mentioned you still want to track down Bryce Barrington, even though the adoptive parents are no longer requiring it."

"It's the right thing to do. I'm seeking a private adoption, so the rules are somewhat less stringent than with a public one, but I still think I should do everything in my power to notify the baby's father of what I'm doing. If I'm unable to find him after giving it my best try I'll be able to proceed with the adoption with a clear conscious."

"That sounds best."

"How's your other project coming along?" Willow asked. "The one to help Burt get his house back?"

"We still have some kinks to work out, but it's coming along. We hope he'll be back in his house before the New Year."

"It's really nice how you and Cody have gone out of your way to help everyone. Not a lot of people would have done that. Most would have stood back and let us all be tossed out in the cold whether we had anywhere to go or not."

"We try to do what we can."

Willow's expression grew serious. "I hope I'm in a position to help others the way you've helped me someday."

I didn't respond. Alex returned to the room with the boxes Tara wanted and Willow and Alex turned their attention to unpacking the last of the inventory, including the bottle of peppermint syrup.

******

Later that morning, Cody came by to let me know we'd be meeting Finn in his office at noon. That worked out for me because I could take my lunch then, and for Cody as well, because he had work he needed to finish at the newspaper and supplies he needed to pick up for the Christmas Eve party that morning.

At Finn's office we gathered around his desk and let him get started. "I spoke to the officer who arrested Bryce after the fight with a man named Cliff Peterman. It seems Bryce had been asking around about Peterman since arriving in Homer, and from what I've been told, he isn't the sort to take kindly to anyone messing around in his personal affairs."

"Bryce must have tracked him to the bar, which angered him," I suggested.

"It does sound as if Bryce confronted Peterman in the bar, which led to the fight. Both men ended up in jail. Peterman is still there, but Bryce, who didn't have a record, was released a few days later."

"I don't suppose the officer knows where Bryce is now?" I asked.

"He didn't, but he said Bryce had adequate cash to leave town."

"What do we know about Peterman?" Cody asked.

Finn shifted in his seat before he answered. "He moved to Homer eight years ago after spending several years in the San Juan Islands. He's been referred to as a bully, has strong opinions, and is likely to engage in physical altercations with anyone who disagrees with or challenges him. The officer indicated Peterman has been in and out of jail for most of his adult life."

I immediately wondered if the fact that Peterman had once lived in the islands was relevant. "Do we know why Bryce was looking for him in the first place?" I asked.

"I believe we do," Finn confirmed. "Buck Barrington died eight years ago as the result of an injury he sustained while intervening in a liquor store robbery. There were no witnesses except for the clerk, who also died, and the image picked up by the security camera was grainy. There were a lot of folks in the area, including the resident deputy at the time, who thought the man whose blurry image was caught on camera was Cliff Peterman, but there wasn't enough evidence to arrest him. He disappeared shortly afterward."

"So Bryce really came to Madrona to find the man who killed his grandfather," I hypothesized.

"It seems that may be exactly why he was here. During the bar fight, Bryce goaded Peterman into admitting he'd been responsible for his grandfather's death in front of witnesses. He's being held on other outstanding warrants while the matter is investigated."

"I guess that makes sense, but Bryce found Peterman and was arrested for his efforts. Peterman is still in jail, so where's Bryce?" I asked.

"At the Inn," Finn said.

"*Our* Iinn?" I asked.

"I received a phone call from Jennifer Conroy shortly before you arrived. She told me Bryce showed up this morning only to let her know he'd done what he'd come to the island to do and would be on his way. He plans to leave on the three o'clock ferry. If Ms. Wood wants to speak to him she'd best do it now."

I stood up in preparation for heading back to the bookstore to speak to Willow. "Why didn't you just lead with that?"

"I thought it was important you had the whole story."

Cody drove me back to the bookstore, where I pulled Willow aside and told her what I knew. It was after one o'clock, so she'd need to make a quick decision about how to proceed. She still said she wanted to speak to Bryce, so I drove her to the Inn.

Jennifer called up to Bryce's room and told him he had a visitor. When he came down the stairs and saw Willow the look on his face confirmed, at least to me, that he hadn't seen her on the island or known she was pregnant. He pulled her into the dining area, which was empty. I watched as he hugged her, then asked her a question. She nodded, and he touched her stomach. She said whatever she intended and he kissed her, then signed the document, which she'd brought with her.

Willow hugged Bryce again, then headed back to me.

"So?" I asked.

"He was naturally surprised, but he didn't have a problem with the concept of adoption. Neither of us is interested in pursuing a relationship and Bryce made it very clear he isn't ready to be a father. We're just getting started in life and have no way to care for a child even if we wanted to try. I never expected he'd want the baby, but I'm glad I had the chance to tell him that he was going to be a father."

"And he wants you to go through with the adoption?"

"He said he'd leave all decisions regarding the baby to me. He's leaving on the next ferry and flying out of Seattle tomorrow. He's on his way home to Chicago to try to work things out with his father. I wish him all the best."

I took Willow's hand. "Do you want to go back to the bookstore?"

Willow smiled. "Of course. Santa needs his elf."

Chapter 14

Saturday, December 23

"Don't be nervous, Miss Cait," eight-year-old Hannah said to me as I stood frozen in fear as the auditorium filled up.

"I'm not nervous," I lied.

"Then how come you're biting your lip so hard it's bleeding?"

I licked my lip, then grimaced. Hannah was right; I'd bitten my lip hard enough to draw blood. You'd think after three years I'd be used to this by now. "Can you go find Cody for me?" I asked Hannah.

"Okay." Hannah put her small hand in mine. "Just remember, Jesus will be happy we're here to celebrate his birth even if we do mess up."

I hugged Hannah. "Thank you. I know you're right. I just need to breathe."

"Yes, ma'am. Mama tells me that same thing whenever I have a math test at school."

Hannah left to find Cody and I looked back toward the audience. Maggie, Father Kilian, Marley, my mom, Finn and Siobhan, Danny and a blonde I didn't recognize, Cassie and her new boyfriend, and even Aiden in a wheelchair, were seated in the first row. Behind them, Tara, Parker, and Amy were next to Willow, Alex, and Balthazar. It did my heart good to see Willow relaxed and smiling despite the challenges of the past month. I noticed Mr. Parsons sitting with Burt and Francine several rows back, and even Bella and Tansy were in the audience, which was a first as far as I knew. I couldn't help but feel happy when I saw all my friends, family, and neighbors gathered to celebrate the kids and the holiday.

"Hannah said you'd forgotten to breathe." Cody walked up behind me and placed one arm around my waist.

"I had a small panic attack, but I'm better now. I've just been focusing on the depth of love and caring in the audience. Sometimes I forget why we're really here."

"It can be a lot to take in. But everyone in the audience is here for the same thing we are, and no one is looking for a perfect production. I see Willow, Alex, and Balthazar made it."

"They did, and they aren't the only ones." I pointed to the back of the auditorium, where Oliva had just walked in with Rosemary and a dark-haired child I was sure was Hillary. I was certain we'd witnessed a true Christmas miracle when Grayson, a woman, and two young boys walked up and joined them. "Oh my God. He must have told his wife about his daughter."

When the party of seven all took seats together I knew without a doubt that miracles are real if only we believe in their power to heal and bring those who should be together, together.

Chapter 15

Tuesday, January 2

"You know how we said we'd wait until after the New Year to talk about the wedding?" Cody said as he walked up behind me and kissed my neck.

"You want to talk about it now?" I asked as he wrapped his arms around me and pulled me against his chest. We'd just spent the day undecorating both my cabin and Mr. Parsons's house.

"I'm not saying we need to figure out every little detail this moment, but I would like to at least open the discussion. I feel like we're in a good place. Both Willow and Alex have decided to stay on the island until after the baby's born, and Willow has told the Plimptons she isn't willing to sign the adoption papers until then, so she has a chance to see how she feels. I'm still not certain how that will work out, but it feels like things are as they should be."

"I agree."

"Additionally, things are slow at the bookstore and Tara has extra help now that Willow's staying. This feels like a good time for us to take a trip together. I figured if we got away we could talk without interruption or the need to entertain the opinion of others."

I smiled. "That does sound good, but don't you need to stay around to make sure Jack Forrester's development is approved? If it falls through he'll probably end up tossing poor Burt out of his own home again."

"The project isn't due to be voted on until the end of February, so we should be fine. Siobhan knows all the details, so she can keep an eye on things."

"Okay. I'll talk to Tara. As long as she's fine with the idea I am too. Where did you want to go?"

Cody paused. "I want to make a stop in New Orleans to check on a friend who's having a hard time, and then I need to go to Tampa for a couple of days to meet with the man who's coordinating the testing of my training program, but after that we can go wherever you want."

"How about Colorado? I've always wanted to go to Aspen in the winter."

Cody turned me around and looked me in the eye. "A week in a snowed-in cabin with no one around but you and me sounds like the perfect romantic getaway."

I grinned. "And there will be plenty of alone time to practice for the honeymoon as well."

Coming next from Kathi Daley Books

Sample Chapter

Wednesday, December 6

My name is Tess Thomas. I live with my dog, Tilly, in White Eagle, Montana, a small town with a big heart nestled in the arms of the Northern Rocky Mountains. I work for the United States Postal Service, delivering mail to the residents of this close-knit community where, more often than not, the folks you grow up with are the same ones you're destined to grow old with.

"Morning, Tess; morning, Tilly," Hap Hollister greeted us as we delivered not only his mail, but the muffins Hattie Johnson had asked me to drop off when Tilly and I had stopped by Grandma Hattie's Bakeshop earlier that morning.

"Morning, Hap." I handed the tall, thin man with snow-white hair a stack of envelopes, as well as the brown paper bag in which Hattie had packed the muffins.

"Pumpkin?" Hap asked.

"Cranberry. Hattie wanted me to assure you they're fresh."

I watched as Hap peeked in the bag. "How's Hattie's arthritis this morning?"

"She seems to be having a good day. You can go by later and ask her yourself." Odd fact about Hap and Hattie: They used to be married, but they separated a few years ago and moved into separate residences, but now they date.

"I'll do that. Hattie and I are planning to take in a movie at the cinema in Kalispell this evening if the snow holds off. Guess I should firm up a time for us to meet."

"You might want to have a backup plan. With those dark clouds overhead, I have a feeling the storm's going to roll in before nightfall. The Community Church has bingo on Wednesdays, if you can't make it to Kalispell."

"Thanks. I'll keep that in mind. It's been hard to find date-night activities since the cinema in town decided to shut down during the winter."

I slipped my mailbag off my shoulder, being careful not to catch my long, curly brown hair in the strap. "I heard there's a group who want to use the space for community events during the winter, though it seems like a lot of folks in the area have an abundance of ideas but are short on follow-through."

"Sounds about right."

I picked up a stack of Christmas CDs Hap had displayed at the front of the home and hardware store Hap owned and operated and began to sort through them. I know that in the age of iTunes, iPods, and smartphones, CDs are a bit outdated, but if you knew the folks of White Eagle, you'd know a lot of them are pretty outdated as well.

"If nothing works out for tonight you could postpone date night until Friday," I suggested. "We have the tree lighting and there's a holiday special at the diner."

"Nope." Hap shook his head. "That won't due at all. Our agreement clearly states that Hattie is to cook dinner for me every Sunday after church, as well as on the seven major holidays, and in return, I'm to take her out on a proper date I plan and pay for every Wednesday as well as every other Saturday."

I paused and looked at Hap. "Has it ever occurred to you and Hattie to set aside this experiment you're engaged in and get back together full time, like everyone knows you should?"

"Sure." Hap nodded but didn't elaborate.

I wanted to say more, but it really wasn't any of my business, so I set the CDs back in the bin and prepared to leave. "Tilly and I should get going if we want to stay ahead of the storm. Got anything outgoing?"

"Actually, I do." Hap set the muffin he'd been nibbling on on the napkin Hattie had provided. "Just give me a minute to fetch it."

Tilly and I wandered over to the potbellied stove to warm up a spell while we waited for Hap. It wasn't easy being a mail carrier in White Eagle, with subzero temperatures and seasonal snow to contend with. But White Eagle was our home, and as far as Tilly and I were concerned, we wouldn't trade it for all the tropical breezes or big-city amenities in the world.

"Here you go." Hap placed a stack of white envelopes on the counter next to a small pile of fishing supplies.

"You planning on doing some fishing?" I asked as I picked up the envelopes.

"A group of us are fixing to enter the old-timers' ice fishing competition at the Winter Carnival." The Winter Carnival in White Eagle was held every year between Christmas and New Year's. "I haven't been fishing since last year's carnival, so I figured I'd better go through my supplies."

"I know the teams are made up of four men. Harley Newsome passed away this year. Have you found a replacement?"

"I spoke to Pike and he said he'd be happy to fill in."

Pike Porter was White Eagle's oldest resident at ninety-two.

"Are you sure that's a good idea?" I asked.

"Man's old, not dead. He said he wanted to do it and I'm inclined to let him"

I supposed Hap had a point, but I worried about Pike walking around on the ice. Once again, however, what he did was none of my business, so I slipped Hap's outgoing mail into my bag without a word. "I really should get a move on. I'll talk to you tomorrow."

"Have you been by Rita's place?" Hap asked as I turned to the door.

"No, not yet." Rita Carson was the local florist.

"I want to send Hattie a rose. Rita said she'd be getting in a shipment today." Hap handed me a twenty-dollar bill. "If you don't mind passing this along, I'd greatly appreciate it."

"No problem." I slid the currency into my pocket.

"Tell Rita to pick out a good one."

"I will, and I'll make sure she delivers it today."

"Thanks, Tess. See you tomorrow."

I pulled the collar of my jacket around my neck as Tilly and I left Hap's home and hardware store. There were snow flurries in the air, which I knew would precede the storm that approached from the far side of the mountain.

I looked at the red envelope at the top of the pile. "Looks like Pike has a letter today."

Tilly barked once in reply. Pike Porter wasn't only one of Tilly's favorite people, he was one of my favorite people as well.

"Let's finish the rest of the route and circle around toward Pike's last so we can sit and chat for a spell. I want to hear all about his plans for the ice fishing tournament."

Tilly must have figured that was a fine idea because she continued down Main Street, passing the alley that led to Pike's tiny cabin, which shared a lot with Pike's Place, the local saloon, which Pike had once owned but had sold.

The next stop on our journey was Sisters' Diner, the cafe my mom, Lucy Thomas, owned with my aunt, Ruthie Turner. My mom and Aunt Ruthie had decided to buy the diner after my dad passed away and Mom realized she would need to find a way to support herself. Ruthie had worked as a cook for the diner's previous owner, who'd expressed a desire to retire to a warmer climate, so the two sisters had pooled their savings and been making a go of the restaurant ever since.

The wreath someone had hung on the door shifted to the side as Tilly and I entered the entryway of the warm, friendly building. I had to smile as a decorative Rudolph with a flashing nose welcomed diners while "Frosty the Snowman" played in the background.

"I've got Christmas cards." I held up several colorful envelopes as I entered the main dining area.

"Oh, good." Mom clapped her hands in delight. Mom and Aunt Ruthie had come up with the idea of soliciting Christmas cards from customers who had dined with them throughout the year. They planned to hang the cards on the back wall after sorting them by general geographic area. It was a cute idea that would not only brighten the place but would demonstrate the fact that customers who stopped by Sisters; Diner represented visitors from every state, as well as many countries around the world.

"Oh, look," Mom said, waving her arms in the air so her red curls bounced up and down. "We have two from Nevada, one from Florida, four from Utah, and one from Florence, Italy."

"Today was a good haul," I agreed. "And the wall is looking really nice. If this idea continues to catch on, you may need to dedicate two walls to the project next year."

"I've been thinking the same thing." Mom grinned. "In fact, with the abundance of international cards that have arrived in the past week, I'm considering changing the theme of this year's tree from Homespun Christmas to Christmas Around the World."

"That would be fun. Maybe you could find ornaments representing all the countries you get cards from, like the Eiffel Tower and the Leaning Tower of Pisa."

"Exactly. Did you notice whether Millie had her novelty ornaments out yet?" Millie Martin owned a home and decorating store at the other end of the row of mom-and-pop shops lining the town's main thoroughfare.

"I didn't notice them when I stopped by to deliver her mail, but I wasn't looking for them either. I guess you can call to ask her. If nothing else, she may be able to special order the kinds of ornaments you're looking for."

"That's a good idea."

"So what are we talking about?" Aunt Ruthie asked after she finished ringing up the customer she'd been dealing with and joined us.

"Ornaments from around the world," Mom answered.

"Did you ask Tess if Millie has her specialty ornaments out?" Ruthie asked.

"She did and I hadn't noticed," I answered in my mom's stead. "She did have baby's first Christmas ornaments displayed near the counter if you want to send something to Johnny."

"The baby won't be born until January, so baby's first Christmas would technically be next year," Aunt Ruthie pointed out. "Still, I'd like to send something special because they're having a girl. I'm hoping they'll name her after me. She's my first granddaughter, you know."

"I'm sure Johnny will take your request into consideration when it comes time to name his daughter." I paused and glanced out the window. "Storm is coming; I'd best be on my way." I turned and looked at my mom. "Dinner on Sunday?"

"Of course, dear. I'll make a pot roast."

Tilly and I left the diner, but not before Aunt Ruthie slipped Tilly a bite of something she'd smuggled from the kitchen. I tried to dissuade Ruthie from feeding Tilly table scraps, but she liked to be sure those who came into the diner were well fed whether they be the customers she served or the four-legged visitors like Tilly, who were only passing by.

The flurries that had been lingering throughout the day were beginning to intensify by the time Tilly and I made our way to the far end of town and crossed the street to start back toward the gazebo, where I'd left my Jeep. I usually liked to say hi to those I served, but given the weather, I realized I might want to speed things up a bit if I didn't want to get caught in a whiteout.

I managed to stick with the plan while delivering mail to Pete's Pets, Sue's Sewing Nook, the Moosehead Bar and Grill, Mel's Meat Locker, and even Rita's shop, Coming Up Daisies, but the moment I entered the Book Boutique, my best friend Bree Price's bookstore, I knew I'd lose my momentum.

"Please tell me you're coming to book club tonight," Bree said the moment Tilly and I entered the cheerily decorated store.

"Tilly and I will be there," I confirmed over the sound of Christmas carols.

"Good." Bree nervously ran her hands down the sides of her dark green angora sweater dress in a gesture I had come to recognize as the prelude to her relaying information she knew I might not want to hear.

"Is there something on your mind?" I asked.

"No." Bree shook her head, but I noticed she was trying hard not to look me in the eye.

"Are you sure?" I asked persuasively.

"Nothing's wrong, but there are some new members joining us tonight. I figured I should let you know so you could wear something nice."

I frowned. "Nice?"

Bree tucked a lock of her perfectly straight, waist-length blond hair behind one ear. "I just figured you might want to make a good first impression because both new members are male, single, and gorgeous. Based on what I know of them, either would make a good match for you."

I lifted one brow. "We've discussed this. I don't do blind dates. Not for anyone and not for any reason."

"It's not a blind date," Bree insisted. "It's just book club, but it seems silly not to put forth a little effort with your appearance. You're going to be twenty-eight on your next birthday. Don't you think it's time to settle down?"

"If by settle down you mean get married, no. Tilly and I are quite happy living on our own. You promised you'd stop with all the matchmaking and I expect you to keep your promise."

"I know," Bree replied. "I just want you to be as happy as Donny and me."

Donny Dunlap was my ex, who I'd dumped after I realized he paid a lot more attention to Bree than he ever paid to me. I know Bree felt bad about basically stealing my guy, but the truth of the matter was I was never really in to Donny all that much, and I was fine with the way things had worked out. Still, Bree, being Bree, wasn't going to fully enjoy her relationship with Donny until I met and fell in love with someone she felt was perfect for me.

"Storm's coming so I need to get going. I'll be at book club, but only if you promise to lay off the matchmaking."

Bree paused.

"Promise me."

"Okay," Bree grudgingly agreed. "Have you been to the police station?"

"No, not yet. Why?"

"Can you drop this book off for your brother? I told him I'd deliver it, but you're going to be stopping in anyway, so…"

"Yeah." I reached out a hand. "I'll make sure Mike gets it."

I had just left the Book Boutique and Tilly and I were heading to our next stop when a bright green sports car whizzed by, splashing sludge on both of us. "Damn it all to hell," I said before I could suppress the curse. "There's no way Fantasia didn't do that on purpose."

Tilly shook the sludge from her fur and barked in agreement.

Fantasia Wade was a twenty-eight-year-old gold digger and former classmate of mine who'd recently married seventy-nine-year-old Austin Wade, the oldest son of one of the town founders and one of the richest men in town. In the year the pair had been married, Fantasia had managed to burn through an impressive amount of his money, which left me wondering when Austin would wise up and put his young bride on a budget.

Given the fact that I had sludge running down my cheek, I turned around and headed back to the bookstore, where I knew Bree would let me clean up in her bathroom.

"What on earth happened to you?" Bree asked when I walked back into her store just a minute after having left.

"Fantasia."

Bree rolled her eyes. "Talk about letting money go to your head. Now that she's married to Austin Wade she seems to think the rules of common courtesy don't apply to her."

"She always has been full of herself. I'll just be a minute."

I tried not to let my anger boil over as I washed my face and used a paper towel to wipe the dirt from my jacket. There were just some people who were born thinking they were better than everyone else and Fantasia was one of them. Of course, the fact that she was drop-dead gorgeous seemed to fuel her superiority complex. It's hard to tell someone who's head cheerleader, homecoming queen, and the most popular girl in school that she's no better than you and make her believe it.

Tilly and I tried to put our little incident with Queen Wade behind us as we finished our route. By the time I'd made my way back to the starting point, where I'd left my Jeep, the sky had darkened. I figured Tilly and I would just drive over to Pike's, so I loaded her in the cargo area, made a U-turn, and headed back to the cabin where White Eagle's oldest resident lived. My route had taken longer than I'd planned, so I wouldn't have as long to chat with Pike as I'd like, but he only received mail a couple of times a month, so when I had a reason to stop in, we generally took it.

"Pike," I called as I rapped on the door.

When there was no answer, Tilly used a paw to scratch at the door.

"Pike, it's Tess and Tilly," I called again.

Still no answer.

I looked down at Tilly. "I guess he's out."

Tilly barked and scratched at the door again. Normally, Tilly wasn't quite so insistent, so I knocked one more time for good measure before slipping the letter under the door and turning away to head back to the Jeep.

Tilly remained at the door rather than following. "Come along, Tilly. Pike's not home."

Tilly barked.

"I know you were looking forward to a visit, but we'll have to come back another day. Maybe tomorrow."

Tilly lay down on the front stoop as if to communicate that she would wait.

"It's snowing and it's almost dark. We can't just stand here waiting for Pike to come home. We still need to make dinner and get cleaned up before book club. Now come along."

Tilly is a sweet and obedient dog who always responds to my requests, so I wasn't sure why she was being so stubborn now. I walked back over to the stoop to give her a gentle shove in the right direction when I heard a tiny sound coming from the other side of the door. I knocked once more but still got no answer. Tilly barked and continued scratching at the door.

"Is Pike in trouble? Do you think we should check on him?"

Once again, Tilly barked.

I reached for the knob and turned it. It was unlocked, so I pushed the door open.

The first thing I noticed was a pile of fishing supplies that must have at one time been on the table were now on the floor. The next thing was a tiny orange-striped kitten was tangled up in a piece of fishing line, which had gotten caught on a nearby table leg. "I suppose you're responsible for Pike's fishing supplies being on the floor."

"Meow."

"Hang on. I have a knife in my Jeep. I'll get it and cut you free."

Tilly stayed with the kitten while I ran back to get the knife. The poor baby was tangled up pretty good. I was going to need to work carefully to get him free without injuring him. It took a good fifteen minutes to finally work him loose, but eventually, I was able to gather him up in my hands. I noticed the poor thing had a nasty-looking cut on one leg.

"Looks like we'll need to stop by to visit Doc Baker," I said to Tilly.

As soon as the kitten was free, Tilly had trotted over to the bedroom door and begun scratching at it.

I crossed the room, knocked on the door, and called Pike's name. There was still no answer, but

Tilly seemed frantic, so I slowly opened the door. "Pike?" I said as I set the kitten down and hurried inside the room. I bent down next to Pike's lifeless body to check for a pulse, but when I noticed the blood on the back of his shirt I knew he was dead.

I picked up the kitten, called to Tilly, and headed back to my Jeep. I called my brother Mike, who told me to wait for him. The sky was almost completely dark by this point, so I turned on my headlights so I wouldn't feel quite so alone and isolated.

I knew I should call Bree to tell her I wasn't going to make it to book club despite my promise to do so, but she'd want a full explanation and ask a lot of questions, and I didn't think I was quite ready to talk about what I'd seen. Still, I didn't want her worrying about me, so I sent a quick text to let her know something had come up and I'd speak to her the following day.

When Mike arrived, he told me to stay put while he went inside. The kitten seemed to be in a playful mood despite his injured leg and Tilly appeared to adore him, so I let the antics of the animals distract me from what was going on inside. After twenty minutes or so, Mike came out of the cabin and approached the Jeep. He slid into the passenger seat and turned me toward him.

"Tell me exactly what occurred leading up to your finding Pike dead on his bedroom floor," Mike said.

"Tilly and I came by to drop off his mail. We were going to stop to chat for a bit. When Pike didn't answer the door, I figured he'd gone out, although I should have realized right away that he never went out when it was snowing."

"And after you arrived?" Mike encouraged.

"I knocked a couple more times and was going to leave, but Tilly wouldn't budge from the front porch. I wanted to check to make sure Pike was okay. I guess he wasn't."

"Did you see anyone else in the area?"

I shook my head. "It was already starting to get dark when we arrived, but I didn't see anyone. Pike's Place opened at two. You can ask whoever's tending bar tonight if they saw or heard anything."

"I'll do that. It's been snowing all day. Did you notice footprints or tire tracks?"

"No. It was snowing hard when I got here. I'm sure any prints that might have been there have been covered by now. Who do you think did this?"

Mike frowned. "I wish I knew. Pike was shot in the back with a small-caliber weapon. I doubt he saw it coming." Mike glanced to the cabin, then back to me. "I noticed fishing supplies scattered across the floor."

"Pike was entering the old-timers' ice fishing competition with Hap this year. I guess he must have been going through his things before whoever killed him arrived. I think the kitten may be responsible for everything being on the floor."

"Okay. I'm going to be here for a while, so you may as well head home. I'll call you if I have any additional questions."

"Okay." I wiped away a tear that had slipped down my cheek. Pike was an old man I spoke to every couple of weeks and whose company I enjoyed, but I didn't know him well. Still, I knew his death would leave a hole in my life. "You need to catch whoever did this."

"Don't worry." Mike squeezed my hand. "I will."

I headed to Doc Baker's. I could probably fix up the kitten's leg with items I had in my cabin, but I wanted to make sure it didn't get infected. I pulled up in front of the veterinary clinic, parked in an empty space, picked up the kitten, and got out of my Jeep. The snow had gotten harder and the lights in the clinic were off, so I went to the front door of the house. Everyone knew if you had an animal emergency and it was after regular hours to go to the front door and Doc Baker would take care of whatever you needed.

I knocked, and Tilly sat down next to me and waited. I could see lights coming on as someone made their way through the house. I cuddled the kitten to my chest while I waited for Doc Baker to make his way to the front of the huge house.

I was prepared with a smile and a greeting but froze the minute the door opened to reveal not a sixty-eight-year-old veterinarian in a white dress shirt but the most perfect man I'd ever seen wearing a towel around his neck and no shirt at all.

"You don't look like the pizza delivery guy." The man seemed as surprised to see me as I was to see him.

"And you don't look like Doc Baker." I couldn't help but stare at the absolutely gorgeous man wearing nothing but faded blue jeans.

He turned around, took a few steps inside, then returned to the door while pulling a T-shirt over his head of thick brown hair. "Sorry about that. I'd just gotten out of the shower when the pizza deliver guy called to let me know he was on his way." He looked at a point over my head. "In fact, there he is now."

"Is Doc Baker here?" I asked, uncertain how else to respond to this absurd situation.

"Doc Baker is my uncle and he's retired. I bought his practice. My name is Brady Baker. Why don't you come on in? I'll pay the pizza guy and then we can take a look at your kitten."

I hesitated, but I really wanted to have the kitten's leg looked at, and the Baker Veterinary Clinic was the only one in town. "Can Tilly come in as well?" I nodded toward the dog sitting next to me.

"Absolutely. If you head straight back, you'll see the door to the clinic on your left."

"I know where it is."

"Great. It's unlocked. Go ahead and wait for me there."

I fought the urge to flee as I slowly walked down the well-lit hallway. To be honest, I couldn't explain where the urge to abandon my mission and take the side exit out to my Jeep came from; maybe I'd simply been thrown for a loop when a gorgeous man close to my own age answered the door instead of the old friend I'd been expecting.

I entered the clinic and set the kitten on the exam table, then motioned for Tilly to sit down nearby. The kitten was favoring the injured leg but didn't appear to be in much pain, so I hoped the injury was minor and wouldn't require stitches or any other equally expensive procedure. I made decent money as a postal worker, but my Jeep was ancient and my cabin old and often in need of repair, and it seemed I was always having a hard time keeping up with the extra expenses. I leaned a hip against the table where I'd placed the kitten and gently played with him while we waited. After a few minutes, Dr. Hunk joined me, fully dressed in jeans, the T-shirt he'd slipped into at the door, and tennis shoes. His hands were free of pizza, so I assumed he'd dropped his dinner off in the kitchen before heading to the clinic. I felt bad he'd have to eat cold food but not bad enough to leave until I had the kitten's leg looked at.

"What do we have here, little fellow?" the man I couldn't seem to think of as Doc Baker asked.

"Mcow."

Blue eyes met my brown eyes. "What's his name?"

"Name?" I asked.

"The kitten. What's his name?"

"Oh. I don't know. I just found him a little while ago. He was tangled up in fishing line. You can see he cut his leg. It doesn't look all that deep, but I wanted to be sure."

"It's always a good idea to err on the side of caution. I don't think he needs stitches."

"That's wonderful," I mumbled as I said a silent prayer of thanks.

"I'll clean him up and bandage the wound. It won't take long."

"Can I stay in here with him?" I asked.

"I don't see why not." He turned to collect the things he'd need. "I take it the dog is yours?"

"Tilly."

Tilly barked once when she heard her name. The new doc smiled, which caused a fluttering in my stomach I hadn't felt for a very long time.

"So, if this is Tilly, you must be Tess."

I frowned. "I am. How did you know?"

"I've heard all about you."

Great. "From who?" I had a feeling I already knew.

"From several people, actually, but most of my knowledge came from the pretty blonde who owns the bookstore."

"The pretty blonde is my soon-to-be ex-best friend, Bree. Please ignore everything she told you. For some reason she feels it's her mission in life to fix me up with every even remotely eligible man who comes into town."

He chuckled. "I see. I guess that explains the rather long interview she conducted while she rang up my books." He handed me the kitten. "Here we go. He should be fine, but why don't you bring him back tomorrow for a quick look? He's a little on the young side to be away from his mama, so I'll give you some formula and bottles to supplement his food as well. You should be able to wean him off the formula in a couple of weeks."

"Okay. And thank you. I'm sorry I interrupted your dinner."

"It's not a problem."

"How much do I owe you?"

He paused. He lifted a dark, bushy brow that perfectly framed his bright blue eyes. "How about dinner?"

"You want me to buy you dinner?"

"No. I want you to share what's sure to be a cold pizza with me."

"Why?" I blurted out before I could consider my answer.

"Because I hate to eat alone and would enjoy the company."

I hesitated.

"It's just pizza. I promise."

"Okay," I agreed. "I guess I have time for a quick slice of cold pizza."

We returned to the house, and he led us to the kitchen, where a beautiful German shepherd was waiting.

"Tess, Tilly. Meet Tracker."

Tilly walked over to the dog, who seemed to be waiting for some sort of a cue from the vet.

"At ease," he said, at which point Tracker began wagging his tail.

"At ease? Is the dog in the military?"

"No. But I used to be, so when I trained him, I used commands familiar to me. *At ease* means it's fine to chill because there isn't a job to do. Tracker isn't a military dog, but he was trained in search and rescue. I have a meeting next week with the local S&R team to see if they have a space for us."

"I'm sure they'll be thrilled to have you."

Tilly sniffed Tracker until she was satisfied he wasn't a threat, then was content to lay down on the rug in front of the brick fireplace, while Tracker settled onto a dog bed nearby. I set the kitten down beside Tilly because they seemed to have bonded and I didn't want him to be afraid of the new surroundings. Of course, the kitten decided it was time to play and not rest and immediately started running around the room, attacking every dust ball he could find.

"Sorry, I guess he's a bit wound up," I apologized.

"I'm glad to see the leg isn't slowing him down."

"He really is a whirlwind of energy," I agreed. "Which is probably how he got tangled in the fishing line in the first place." I chuckled as he jumped into the air and then did a complete three sixty before landing.

"I think you're going to have your hands full with this one. Wine?" he offered.

"I should stick to water. I still need to drive home and it's snowing pretty hard. I'll need to be alert."

He set a bottle of water in front of each of us, along with the pan of pizza he'd warmed momentarily in the oven.

"How long have you lived here?" I asked. "I wasn't even aware Doc Baker had retired."

"Just a couple of weeks. My uncle's been talking about retiring for quite some time, but he didn't want to leave until he was sure there was someone to take over the practice. At first I wasn't sure I wanted it, but after some soul-searching following a broken engagement, I decided maybe moving to White Eagle was a good idea after all."

"I'm sorry to hear about your breakup, but I'm happy to have someone to take over the practice. Your uncle was the only vet in town."

"That was why he waited so long to retire."

I glanced at the kitten, who was now pouncing on Tilly's head. Being the patient dog she was, she just lay there and took whatever abuse the kitten dished out until he knocked a roll of gauze off the table and became hopelessly entangled once again.

"Looks like we have another tangle emergency." I laughed.

"Maybe that's what you should name him: Tangle," he suggested.

"I was thinking of something with a Christmas feel to it, like Mistletoe."

"Mistletoe is a good name now, but you may not feel the same when it's no longer Christmas. How about combining Tangle with Mistletoe?"

"Combining?"

"Tangletoe."

I laughed again. "That's a ridiculous name."

He grinned, looking me in the eye. "But you love it, right?"

I grinned back. "Actually, I kinda do."

Recipes

Peanut Bunches—submitted by Taryn Lee
Mama's Fruitcake—submitted by Nina Banks
Christmas Jam Cake—submitted by Jeannie Daniels
Snowballs—submitted by Pamela Curran
Rum Bundt Cake—submitted by Vivian Shane
Peanut Butter Christmas Mice—submitted by Robin Coxon

Peanut Bunches

Submitted by Taryn Lee

Good for cookie exchanges.

1 cup sugar
⅓ cup evaporated milk
¼ cup (½ stick) butter
¼ cup crunchy peanut butter
½ tsp. vanilla
2 cups quick-cooking oats
½ cup peanuts
½ cup semisweet chocolate chips

Line cookie sheet with parchment paper. Mix sugar, milk, and butter in a small saucepan. Bring mixture to a boil. Take off heat and stir in peanut butter and vanilla until blended. Mix in remaining ingredients. Drop tablespoon-size mixture onto cookie sheet. If your mixture becomes too stiff add in another couple of drops of milk. Refrigerate for 30 minutes or until firm.

Makes about 2 dozen bunches.

Mama's Fruitcake

Submitted by Nina Banks

This always made the house smell so good, but was a long time making. This recipe was handed down to me by my grandmother, who got it from her mother.

Combine:
1 cup dates
1 cup raisins
⅔ cup butter
1¼ cups brown sugar
¼ cup dark molasses
1½ cups hot water

Boil gently for 3 minutes. Cool in large mixing bowl.
Beat in 2 eggs.

Add:
2 cups canned fruit (fruitcake mix)
1 cup chopped walnuts

Sift together:

3 cups flour
½ tsp. nutmeg
½ tsp. cinnamon
1 tsp. soda
1 tsp. salt
1 tsp. baking powder

Add to fruitcake mix, beat well, and pour in 9-inch tube pan, lined with greased wax paper.
Bake at 275 degrees for 2½ hours. Cool 10 minutes, then remove from pan.

Cool thoroughly, dip a piece of clean cloth in rum, etc., and place in center of fruitcake, dip another piece into rum and place on top, wrap in foil, and store in cool place. Once a week, repeat above for 3 to 4 weeks to age. Will store up to 6 weeks.

Christmas Jam Cake

Submitted by Jeannie Daniel

This is a family recipe we use a lot at the holidays, using my daughter's homemade blackberry jam.

2 cups sugar
1½ cups margarine or unsalted butter
1 cup blackberry jam
1 cup strawberry jam
1⅓ cups buttermilk
4 cups flour
2 tsp. baking soda
1 tbs. allspice
1 tbs. cinnamon
6 egg whites
1 cup raisins

Cream sugar and margarine in bowl until light and fluffy. Mix in the jams and buttermilk. Mix flour, baking soda, allspice, and cinnamon; once mixed, add to creamed mixture. Fold in unbeaten egg whites and raisins. Pour into 3 greased and floured 9-inch pans. Bake at 350 degrees for 25 to 30 minutes or until it tests done. Frost with favorite icing.

Snowballs

Submitted by Pamela Curran

These came from a former student's mother one Christmas.

¼ cup butter
½ cup sugar
1 egg yolk
½ cup crushed pineapple, drained well
½ cup chopped nuts
66 vanilla wafers (1 box)
2 cups whipping cream
Coconut

Mix first 5 ingredients. Put down one vanilla wafer, top with pineapple mixture, a wafer, more pineapple mixture, and a third wafer. Repeat until all wafers are used. Refrigerate layered wafers overnight. Whip the cream until thick, sweeten with some sugar. Frost the wafers with the cream and sprinkle with coconut. Serve chilled. Keep unused snowballs refrigerated.

Makes 22 snowballs.

Rum Bundt Cake

Submitted by Vivian Shane

Cake:
1 cup chopped pecans
18½-oz. pkg. yellow cake mix with pudding
3 eggs
½ cup cold water
⅓ cup vegetable oil
½ cup dark rum

Glaze:
1 stick butter
¼ cup water
1 cup sugar
⅓ cup dark rum

Preheat oven to 325 degrees. Grease and flour Bundt pan. Sprinkle the nuts in the bottom of the pan. Mix cake ingredients together and pour over nuts. Bake for an hour. Cool and invert onto a serving plate.

For glaze, melt butter in saucepan, stir in sugar and water. Boil for 5 minutes, stirring constantly. Remove from heat and stir in rum.

Prick the top of the cake with a fork and spoon/brush glaze evenly over top and sides. Allow the cake to absorb the glaze, then repeat until glaze is used up.

Peanut Butter Christmas Mice

Submitted by Robin Coxon

½ cup butter, room temperature
2 cups creamy peanut butter
½ cup packed light brown sugar
½ cup white sugar
1 egg
1 tsp. vanilla extract
½ tsp. baking soda
1½ cups all-purpose flour
1 cup peanut halves
¼ cup green candy sprinkles
60 3-inch pieces red shoestring licorice

In a large bowl, combine butter and peanut butter; beat until creamy. Add brown and white sugar until fluffy. Beat in egg, vanilla extract, and baking soda until well blended. With mixer on low, mix in flour just until blended. Cover and chill for 1 hour, or until firm.

Preheat oven to 350 degrees.

Shape 1 level tablespoon dough into 1-inch balls. Taper each ball at one end into a teardrop shape. Press the sides of the dough in to raise the "backs" of the mice, as dough will spread slightly during baking.

Gently push 2 peanut halves in each shape to resemble "mouse ears" and 2 pieces of green candy for eyes. With a toothpick, make a hole ½-inch deep in the tail ends.

Bake in preheated oven for 8 to 10 minutes, or until firm.

Transfer to a cooling rack and insert licorice pieces as tails.

Books by Kathi Daley

Come for the murder, stay for the romance.

Zoe Donovan Cozy Mystery:

Halloween Hijinks
The Trouble With Turkeys
Christmas Crazy
Cupid's Curse
Big Bunny Bump-off
Beach Blanket Barbie
Maui Madness
Derby Divas
Haunted Hamlet
Turkeys, Tuxes, and Tabbies
Christmas Cozy
Alaskan Alliance
Matrimony Meltdown
Soul Surrender
Heavenly Honeymoon
Hopscotch Homicide
Ghostly Graveyard
Santa Sleuth
Shamrock Shenanigans
Kitten Kaboodle
Costume Catastrophe
Candy Cane Caper
Holiday Hangover
Easter Escapade
Camp Carter
Trick or Treason
Reindeer Roundup – *December 2017*

Zimmerman Academy The New Normal
Ashton Falls Cozy Cookbook

Tj Jensen Paradise Lake Mysteries by Henery Press:

Pumpkins in Paradise
Snowmen in Paradise
Bikinis in Paradise
Christmas in Paradise
Puppies in Paradise
Halloween in Paradise
Treasure in Paradise
Fireworks in Paradise
Beaches in Paradise – *June 2018*

Whales and Tails Cozy Mystery:

Romeow and Juliet
The Mad Catter
Grimm's Furry Tail
Much Ado About Felines
Legend of Tabby Hollow
Cat of Christmas Past
A Tale of Two Tabbies
The Great Catsby
Count Catula
The Cat of Christmas Present
A Winter's Tail
The Taming of the Tabby
Frankencat
The Cat of Christmas Future
The Cat of New Orleans – *February 2018*

Seacliff High Mystery:

The Secret
The Curse
The Relic
The Conspiracy
The Grudge
The Shadow
The Haunting

Sand and Sea Hawaiian Mystery:

Murder at Dolphin Bay
Murder at Sunrise Beach
Murder at the Witching Hour
Murder at Christmas
Murder at Turtle Cove
Murder at Water's Edge
Murder at Midnight

Writers' Retreat Southern Seashore Mystery:

First Case
Second Look
Third Strike
Fourth Victim
Fifth Night – *January 2018*

Rescue Alaska Paranormal Mystery:
Finding Justice

A Tess and Tilly Mystery:
The Christmas Letter – *December 2017*

Road to Christmas Romance:
Road to Christmas Past

USA Today best-selling author, Kathi Daley lives in beautiful Lake Tahoe with her husband Ken. When she isn't writing, she likes spending time hiking the miles of desolate trails surrounding her home. She has authored more than seventy-five books in eight series including: Zoe Donovan Cozy Mysteries, Whales and Tails Island Mysteries, Sand and Sea Hawaiian Mysteries, Tj Jensen Paradise Lake Series, Writers' Retreat Southern Seashore Mysteries, Rescue Alaska Paranormal Mysteries, and Seacliff High Teen Mysteries. Find out more about her books at **www.kathidaley.com**

Stay up to date:
Newsletter, *The Daley Weekly*
http://eepurl.com/NRPDf
Kathi Daley Blog – publishes each Friday
http://kathidaleyblog.com
Webpage – **www.kathidaley.com**
Facebook at Kathi Daley Books –
www.facebook.com/kathidaleybooks
Kathi Daley Teen –
www.facebook.com/kathidaleyteen
Kathi Daley Books Group Page –
https://www.facebook.com/groups/569578823146850/
E-mail – **kathidaley@kathidaley.com**
Goodreads –
https://www.goodreads.com/author/show/7278377.Kathi_Daley
Twitter at Kathi Daley@kathidaley –
https://twitter.com/kathidaley

Amazon Author Page –
https://www.amazon.com/author/kathidaley
BookBub –
https://www.bookbub.com/authors/kathi-daley
Pinterest – **http://www.pinterest.com/kathidaley/**

Made in the USA
Columbia, SC
29 September 2018